THE HOUSE OF THE WOLF

By STANLEY J. WEYMAN, *author of* "*The King's Stratagem*," *etc.* . . . .

NEW YORK AND LONDON
STREET & SMITH, PUBLISHERS

CONTENTS.

INTRODUCTION.

THE following is a modern English version of a curious French memoir, or fragment of autobiography, apparently written about the year 1620 by Anne, Vicomte de Caylus, and brought to this country — if, in fact, the original ever existed in England — by one of his descendants, after the Revocation of the Edict of Nantes. This Anne, we learn from other sources, was a principal figure at the court of Henry IV, and, therefore, in August, 1572, when the adventures here related took place, he and his two younger brothers, Marie and Croisette, who shared with him the honor and the danger, must have been little more than boys. From the tone of his narrative, it appears that, in reviving old recollections, the veteran renewed his youth also, and though his story throws no fresh light upon the history of the time, it seems to possess some human interest.

THE HOUSE OF THE WOLF.

CHAPTER I.

WARE WOLF!

I HAD afterward such good reason to look back upon and remember the events of that afternoon, that Catherine's voice seems to ring in my brain even now. I can shut my eyes and see again, after all these years, what I saw then — just the blue summer sky, and one gray angle of the keep, from which a fleecy cloud was trailing like the smoke from a chimney. I could see no more because I was lying on my back, my head resting on my hands. Marie and Croisette, my brothers, were lying by me in exactly the same posture, and a few yards away on the terrace, Catherine was sitting on a stool Gil had brought out for her. It was the second Thursday in August, and hot. Even the jackdaws were silent. I had almost fallen asleep, watching my cloud grow longer and longer, and thinner and thinner, when Croisette, who cared for heat no more than a lizard, spoke up sharply. "Mademoiselle," he said, "why are you watching the Cahors road ?"

I had not noticed that she was doing so. But something in the keenness of Croisette's tone, taken perhaps with the fact that Catherine did not at once answer him, aroused me; and I turned to her. And lo! she was blushing in the most heavenly way, and her eyes were full of tears, and she looked at us adorably. And we all three sat up on our elbows, like three puppy dogs, and looked at her. And there was a long silence. And then she said quite simply to us, "Boys, I am going to be married to M. de Pavannes."

I fell flat on my back and spread out my arms. "Oh, mademoiselle!" I cried, reproachfully.

"Oh, mademoiselle!" cried Marie. And he fell flat on his back, and spread out his arms and moaned. He was a good brother, was Marie, and obedient.

And Croisette cried, "Oh, mademoiselle!" too. But he was always ridiculous in his ways. He fell flat on his back, and flopped his arms and squealed like a pig.

Yet he was sharp. It was he who first remembered our duty, and went to Catherine, cap in hand, where she sat half-angry and half-confused, and said with a fine redness in his cheeks, "Mademoiselle de Caylus, our cousin, we give you joy, and wish you long life, and are your servants, and the good friends and aiders of M. de Pavannes in all quarrels, as —"

But I could not stand that. "Not so fast, St. Croix de Caylus," I said, pushing him aside — he was ever getting before me in those days — and taking his place. Then with my best bow I began, "Mademoiselle, we give you joy and long life, and are your servants and the good friends and aiders of M. de Pavannes in all quarrels, as — as —"

"As becomes the cadets of your house," suggested Croisette, softly.

"As becomes the cadets of your house," I repeated. And then Catherine stood up and made me a low bow, and we all kissed her hand in turn, beginning with me and ending with Croisette, as was becoming. Afterward Catherine threw her handkerchief over her face — she was crying — and we three sat down, Turkish fashion, just where we were, and said "Oh, Kit!" very softly.

But presently Croisette had something to add. "What will the Wolf say?" he whispered to me.

"Ah! to be sure!" I exclaimed aloud. I had been thinking of myself before, but this opened quite another window. "What will the vidame say, Kit?"

She dropped her kerchief from her face and turned so pale that I was sorry I had spoken — apart from the kick Croisette gave me. "Is M. de Bezers at his house?" she asked, anxiously.

"Yes," Croisette answered. "He came in last night from St. Antonin, with very small attendance."

The news seemed to set her fears at rest instead of augmenting them, as I should have expected. I suppose they were rather for Louis de Pavannes than for herself. Not unnaturally, too, for even the Wolf could scarcely have found it in his heart to hurt our cousin. Her slight willowy figure, her pale oval face and gentle brown eyes, her pleasant voice, her kindness, seemed to us boys, in those days, to sum up all that was womanly. We could not remember — not even Croisette, the youngest of us, who was seventeen, a year junior to Marie and myself (we were twins) — the time when we had not been in love with her.

But let me explain how we four, whose united ages scarce exceeded seventy years, came to be lounging on the terrace in the holiday stillness of that afternoon. It was the summer of 1572. The great peace, it will be remembered, between the Catholics and the Huguenots had not long been declared; the peace which in a day or two was to be solemnized and, as most Frenchmen hoped, to be cemented by the marriage of Henry of Navarre with Margaret of Valois, the king's sister. The Vicomte de Caylus, Catherine's father and our guardian, was one of the governors appointed to see the peace enforced, the respect in which he was held by both parties — he was a Catholic but no bigot, God rest his soul! — recommending him for this employment. He had therefore gone a week or two before to Bayonne, his province. Most of our neighbors in Quercy were likewise from home, having gone to Paris to be witnesses on one side or the other of the royal wedding. And consequently we young people, not greatly checked by the presence of good-natured, sleepy Madame Claude, Catherine's duenna, were disposed to make the most of our liberty, and to celebrate the peace in our own fashion.

We were country folk. Not one of us had been to Pau, much less to Paris. The vicomte held stricter views than were common then, upon young people's education; and though we had learned to ride and shoot, to use our swords and toss a hawk, and to read and write, we knew little more than Catherine herself of the world; little more of the pleasures and sins of court life, and not one-tenth as much as she did of its graces. Still she had taught us to dance and make a bow. Her presence had softened our manners, and of late we had gained something from the frank companionship of Louis de Pavannes, a Huguenot whom the vicomte had taken prisoner at Moncontour and held to ransom. We were not, I think, mere clownish yokels.

But we were shy. We disliked and shunned strangers. And when old Gil appeared suddenly, while we were still chewing the melancholy cud of Kit's announcement, and cried sepulchrally, "M. le Vidame de Bezers to pay his respects to mademoiselle!" — well, there was something like a panic, I confess!

We scrambled to our feet, muttering, "The Wolf!" The entrance at Caylus is by a ramp rising from the gateway to the level of the terrace. This sunken way is fenced by low walls so that one may not — when walking on the terrace — fall into it. Gil had spoken before his head had well risen to view, and this gave us a moment, just a moment. Croisette made a rush for the doorway into the house, but failed to gain it, and drew himself up behind a buttress of the tower, his finger on his lip. I am slow sometimes, and Marie waited for me, so that we had barely got to our legs — looking, I dare say, awkward and ungainly enough — before the vidame's shadow fell darkly on the ground at Catherine's feet.

"Mademoiselle!" he said, advancing to her through the sunshine, and bending over her slender hand with a magnificent grace that was born of his size and manner combined, "I rode in late last night from Toulouse, and I go to-morrow to Paris. I have but rested and washed off the stains of travel that I may lay my — ah!"

He seemed to see us for the first time and negligently broke off in his compliment, raising himself and saluting us. "Ah," he continued, indolently, "two of the maidens of Caylus, I see. With an odd pair of hands apiece, unless I am mistaken. Why do you not set them spinning, mademoiselle?" and he regarded us with that smile which—with other things as evil—had made him famous.

Croisette pulled horrible faces behind his back. We looked hotly at him, but could find nothing to say.

"You grow red!" he went on, pleasantly—the wretch!—playing with us as a cat does with mice. "It offends your dignity, perhaps, that I bid mademoiselle set you spinning? I now would spin at mademoiselle's bidding, and think it happiness!"

"We are not girls!" I blurted out, with the flush and tremor of a boy's passion. "You had not called my godfather, Anne de Montmorenci, a girl, M. le Vidame!" For though we counted it a joke among ourselves that we all bore girls' names, we were young enough to be sensitive about it.

He shrugged his shoulders. And how he dwarfed us all as he stood there dominating our terrace! "M. de Montmorenci was a man," he said, scornfully. "M. Anne de Caylus is—"

And the villain deliberately turned his great back upon us, taking his seat on the low wall near Catherine's chair. It was clear, even to our vanity, that he did not think us worth another word—that we had passed absolutely from his mind. Madame Claude came waddling out at the same moment, Gil carrying a chair behind her; and we—well we slunk away and sat on the other side of the terrace, whence we could still glower at the offender.

Yet who were we to glower at him? To this day I shake at the thought of him. It was not so much his height and bulk, though he was so big that the clipped pointed fashion of his beard —a fashion then new at court—seemed on him incongruous and effeminate; nor so much the sinister glance of his gray eyes—he had a slight cast in them; nor the grim suavity of his manner, and the harsh threatening voice that permitted of no disguise. It was the sum of these things, the great brutal presence of the man—that was over-powering—that made the great falter and the poor crouch. And then his reputation! Though we knew little of the world's wickedness, all we did know had come to us linked with his name. We had heard of him as a duelist, as a bully, an employer of bravos. At Jarnac he had been the last to turn from the shambles. Men called him cruel and vengeful even for those days—gone by now, thank God! — and whispered his name when they spoke of assassinations, saying commonly of him that he would not blench before a Guise, nor blush before the Virgin.

Such was our visitor and neighbor, Raoul de Mar, Vidame de Bezers. As he sat on the terrace, now eyeing us askance, and now paying Catherine a compliment, I likened him to a great cat before which a butterfly has all unwittingly flirted her prettiness. Poor Catherine! No doubt she had her own reasons for uneasiness, more reasons I fancy than I then guessed; for she seemed to have lost her voice. She stammered and made but poor replies, and Madame Claude being deaf and stupid, and we boys too timid after the rebuff we had experienced to fill the gap, the conversation languished. The vidame was not for his part the man to put himself out on a hot day.

It was after one of these pauses — not the first but the longest — that I started on finding his eyes fixed on mine. More, I shivered. It is hard to describe, but there was a look in the vidame's eyes at that moment which I had never seen before, a look of pain almost; of dumb savage alarm, at any rate. From me they passed slowly to Marie and mutely interrogated him. Then the vidame's glance traveled back to Catherine, and settled on her.

Only a moment before she had been but too

conscious of his presence. Now, as it chanced by
bad luck, or in the course of Providence, something had drawn her attention elsewhere. She
was unconscious of his regard. Her own eyes
were fixed in a far-away gaze. Her color was
high, her lips were parted, her bosom heaved
gently.

The shadow deepened on the vidame's face.
Slowly he took his eyes from hers, and looked
northward also.

Caylus Castle stands on a rock in the middle of
the narrow valley of that name. · The town
clusters about the ledges of the rock so closely
that when I was a boy I could fling a stone clear
of the houses. The hills are scarcely five hundred
yards distant on either side, rising in tamer colors
from the green fields about the brook. It is
possible from the terrace to see the whole valley,
and the road which passes through it lengthwise.
Catherine's eyes were on the northern extremity
of the defile, where the highway from Cahors
descends from the uplands. She had been sitting
with her face turned that way all the afternoon.

I looked that way too. A solitary horseman
was descending the steep track from the hills.

"Mademoiselle!" cried the vidame, suddenly.
We all looked up. His tone was such that the
color fled from Kit's face. There was something
in his voice she had never heard in any voice

before—something that to a woman was like a blow. "Mademoiselle," he snarled, "is expecting news from Cahors, from her lover. I have the honor to congratulate M. de Pavannes on his conquest."

Ah! he had guessed it! As the words fell on the sleepy silence, an insult in themselves, I sprang to my feet, amazed and angry, yet astounded by his quickness of sight and wit. He must have recognized the Pavannes badge at that distance. "M. le Vidame," I said, indignantly—Catherine was white and voiceless—"M. le Vidame—" but there I stopped and faltered, stammering; for behind him I could see Croisette, and Croisette gave me no sign of encouragement or support.

So we stood face to face for a moment; the boy and the man of the world, the stripling and the *roué*. Then the vidame bowed to me in quite a new fashion. "M. Anne de Caylus desires to answer for M. de Pavannes?" he asked, smoothly, with a mocking smoothness.

I understood what he meant; but something prompted me—Croisette said afterward that it was a happy thought, though now I know the crisis to have been less serious than he fancied —to answer, "Nay, not for M. de Pavannes. Rather for my cousin." And I bowed. "I have the honor on her behalf to acknowledge your

congratulations, M. le Vidame. It pleases her
that our nearest neighbor should also be the first
outside the family to wish her well. You have
divined truly in supposing that she will shortly
be united to M. de Pavannes."

I suppose — for I saw the giant's color change
and his lip quiver as I spoke—that his previous
words had been only a guess. For a moment the
devil seemed to be glaring through his eyes, and
he looked at Marie and me as a wild animal at its
keepers. Yet he maintained his cynical politeness in part. "Mademoiselle desires my congratulations?" he said, slowly, laboring with
each word, it seemed. "She shall have them on
the happy day. She shall certainly have them
then. But these are troublous times. And
mademoiselle's betrothed is, I think, a Huguenot,
and has gone to Paris. Paris — well, the air of
Paris is not good for Huguenots, I am told."

I saw Catherine shiver; indeed she was on the
point of fainting. I broke in rudely, my passion
getting the better of my fears. "M. de Pavannes
can take care of himself, believe me," I said
brusquely.

"Perhaps so," Bezers answered, his voice like
the grating of steel on steel. "But at any rate
this will be a memorable day for mademoiselle,
the day on which she receives her first congratulations — she will remember it as long as she lives!

Oh, yes, I will answer for that, M. Anne," he said, looking brightly at one and another of us, his eyes more oblique than ever, "Mademoiselle will remember it, I am sure!"

It would be impossible to describe the devilish glance he flung at the poor sinking girl as he withdrew, the horrid emphasis he threw into those last words, the covert deadly threat they conveyed to the dullest ears. That he went then, was small mercy. He had done all the evil he could do at present. If his desire had been to leave fear behind him, he had certainly succeeded.

Kit, crying softly, went into the house, her innocent coquetry more than sufficiently punished already. And we three looked at one another with blank faces. It was clear that we had made a dangerous enemy, and an enemy at our own gates. As the vidame had said, these were troublous times when things were done to men —ay, and to women and children — which we scarce dare to speak of now. "I wish the vicomte were here," Croisette said, uneasily, after we had discussed several unpleasant contingencies.

"Or even Malines, the steward," I suggested.

"He would not be much good," replied Croisette, "and he is at St. Antonin, and will not be back this week. Father Pierre, too, is at Albi."

"You do not think," said Marie, "that he will attack us?"

"Certainly not!" Croisette retorted, with contempt. "Even the vidame would not dare to do
that in time of peace. Besides, he has not half a
score of men here," continued the lad, shrewdly,
"and counting old Gil and ourselves, we have as
many. And Pavannes always said that three
men could hold the gates at the bottom of the
ramp against a score. Oh, he will not try that!"

"Certainly not!" I agreed. And so we crushed
Marie. "But for Louis de Pavannes—"

Catherine interrupted me. She came out
quickly, looking a different person, her face
flushed with anger, her tears dried.

"Anne!" she cried, imperiously, "what is the
matter down below—will you see?"

I had no difficulty in doing that. All the sounds
of town life came up to us on the terrace. Lounging there we could hear the chaffering over the
wheat measures in the cloisters of the market-
square, the yell of a dog, the voice of a scold, the
church bell, the watchman's cry. I had only to
step to the wall to overlook it all. On this summer afternoon the town had been for the most
part very quiet. If we had not been engaged in
our own affairs we should have taken the alarm
before, remarking in the silence the first begin-
nings of what was now a very respectable tumult.
It swelled louder even as we stepped to the wall.

We could see—a bend in the street laying it

open — part of the vidame's house, the gloomy square hold which had come to him from his mother. His own chateau of Bezers lay far away in Franche Comte, but of late he had shown a preference — Catherine could best account for it, perhaps — for this mean house in Caylus. It was the only house in the town which did not belong to us. It was known as the House of the Wolf, and was a grim stone building surrounding a court-yard. Rows of wolves' heads carved in stone flanked the windows, whence their bare fangs grinned day and night at the church porch opposite.

The noise drew our eyes in this direction, and there, lolling in a window over the door, looking out on the street with a laughing eye, was Bezers himself. The cause of his merriment — we had not far to look for it — was a horseman who was riding up the street under difficulties. He was reining in his steed — no easy task on that steep, greasy pave-ment — so as to present some front to a score or so of ragged knaves who were following close at his heels, hooting and throwing mud and pebbles at him. The man had drawn his sword, and his oaths came up to us, mingled with shrill cries of " *Vive la messe!*" and half-drowned by the clat-tering of the horse's hoofs. We saw a stone strike him in the face, and draw blood, and heard him swear louder than before.

"Oh!" cried Catherine, clasping her hands with a sudden shriek of indignation, "my letter! They will get my letter!"

"Death!" exclaimed Croisette. "She is right! It is M. de Pavannes' courier! This must be stopped! We can not stand this, Anne!"

"They shall pay dearly for it, by our Lady!" I cried, swearing myself. "And in peace time too —the villains! Gil! Francis!" I shouted, "where are you?"

And I looked round for my fowling-piece, while Croisette jumped on the wall, and forming a trumpet with his hands, shrieked at the top of his voice, "Back! he bears a letter from the vicomte!"

But the device did not succeed, and I could not find my gun. For a moment we were helpless, and before I could have fetched the gun from the house, the horseman and the hooting rabble at his heels had turned a corner and were hidden by the roofs.

Another turn, however, would bring them out in front of the gateway, and seeing this we hurried down the ramp to meet them. I stayed a moment to tell Gil to collect the servants, and this keeping me, Croisette reached the narrow street outside before me. As I followed him I was nearly knocked down by the rider, whose face was covered with dirt and blood, while fright had rendered his horse unmanageable. Darting aside I let him pass—he was blinded and could not see me—and then found that Croisette, brave lad, had collared the foremost of the ruffians and was beating him with his sheathed sword, while the rest of the rabble stood back, ashamed, yet sullen, and with anger in their eyes. A dangerous crew, I thought; not townsmen, most of them.

"Down with the Huguenots!" cried one, as I appeared, one bolder than the rest.

"Down with the *canaille!*" I retorted, sternly eyeing the ill-looking ring. "Will you set yourselves above the king's peace, dirt that you are? Go back to your kennels!"

The words were scarcely out of my mouth before I saw that the fellow whom Croisette was punishing had got hold of a dagger. I shouted a warning, but it came too late. The blade fell, and, thanks to God, striking the buckle of the lad's belt, glanced off harmless. I saw the steel flash up again—saw the spite in the man's eyes; but this time I was a step nearer, and before the weapon fell I passed my sword clean through the wretch's body. He went down like a log, Croisette falling with him, held fast by his stiffening fingers.

I had never killed a man before, nor seen a man die, and if I had stayed to think about it I should have fallen sick perhaps. But it was no time for thought, no time for sickness. The crowd were close upon us, a line of flushed threatening faces from wall to wall. A single glance downward told me that the man was dead, and I set my foot upon his neck. "Hounds! Beasts!" I cried, not loudly this time, for though I was like one possessed with rage, it was inward rage. "Go to your kennels! Will you dare to raise a hand against a Caylus? Go! or when the vicomte returns a dozen of you shall hang in the market-place!"

I suppose I looked fierce enough — I know I felt no fear, only a strange exaltation — for they slunk away. Unwillingly, but with little delay, the group melted, Bezers' following — of whom I knew the dead man was one — the last to go. While I still glared at them, lo! the street was empty; the last had disappeared round the bend. I turned to find Gil and half a dozen servants standing with pale faces at my back. Croisette seized my hand with a sob. "Oh, my lord," cried Gil, quaveringly. But I shook one off, I frowned at the other.

"Take up this carrion!" I said, touching it with my foot, "and hang it from the justice-elm. And then close the gates. See to it, knaves, and lose no time."

CHAPTER II.

THE VIDAME'S THREAT.

CROISETTE used to tell a story of the facts, of which I have no remembrance save as a bad dream. He would have it that I left my pallet that night — I had one to myself in the summer, being the eldest, while he and Marie slept on another in the same room — and came to him and awoke him, sobbing and shaking and clutching him, and begging him in a fit of terror not to let me go; and that so I slept in his arms until morning. But as I have said, I do not remember anything of this, only that I had an ugly dream that night, and that when I awoke I was lying with him and Marie, so I can not say whether it really happened.

At any rate, if I had any feeling of the kind it did not last long; on the contrary — it would be idle to deny it — I was flattered by the sudden respect Gil and the servants showed me. What Catherine thought of the matter I could not tell. She had her letter and apparently found it satisfactory. At any rate we saw nothing of her. Madame Claude was busy boiling simples, and ending the messenger's hurts. And it seemed natural that I should take command.

There could be no doubt — at any rate we had
none — that the assault on the courier had taken
place at the vidame's instance. The only wonder
was that he had not simply cut his throat and
taken the letter. But looking back now it seems
to me that grown men mingled some childishness
with their cruelty in those days — days when the
religious wars had aroused our worst passions.
It was not enough to kill an enemy. It pleased
people to make — I speak literally — a football
of his head, to throw his heart to the dogs. And
no doubt it had fallen in with the vidame's grim
humor that the bearer of Pavannes' first love-
letter should enter his mistress' presence bleed-
ing and plastered with mud. And that the riff-
raff about our own gates should have part in the
insult.

Bezers' wrath would be little abated by the
issue of the affair, or the justice I had done on
one of his men. So we looked well to bolts, and
bars, and windows, although the castle is well
nigh impregnable, the smooth rock falling twenty
feet at least on every side from the base of the
walls. The gatehouse, Pavannes had shown us,
might be blown up with gunpowder indeed, but
we prepared to close the iron grating which barred
the way half-way up the ramp. This done, even
if the enemy should succeed in forcing an entrance
he would only find himself caught in a trap — in

a steep, narrow way exposed to a fire from the top of the flanking walls, as well as from the front. We had a couple of culverins, which the vicomte had got twenty years before, at the time of the battle of St. Quentin. We fixed one of these at the head of the ramp, and placed the other on the terrace, where, by moving it a few paces forward, we could train it on Bezers' house, which thus lay at our mercy.

Not that we really expected an attack, but we did not know what to expect or what to fear. We had not ten servants, the vicomte having taken a score of the sturdiest lackeys and keepers to attend him at Bayonne. And we felt immensely responsible. Our main hope was that the vidame would at once go on to Paris, and postpone his vengeance. So again and again we cast longing glances at the House of the Wolf, hoping that each symptom of bustle heralded his departure.

Consequently it was a shock to me, and a great downfall of hopes, when Gil with a grave face came to me on the terrace and announced that . M. le Vidame was at the gate, asking to see mademoiselle.

"It is out of the question that he should see her," the old servant added, scratching his head in grave perplexity.

"Most certainly. I will see him instead," I

answered, stoutly. "Do you leave Francis and another at the gate, Gil. Marie, keep within sight, lad. And let Croisette stay with me."

These preparations made—and they took up scarcely a moment—I met the vidame at the head of the ramp. "Mademoiselle de Caylus," I said, bowing, "is, I regret to say, indisposed to-day, Vidame."

"She will not see me?" he asked, eyeing me very unpleasantly.

"Her indisposition deprives her of the pleasure," I answered with an effort. He was certainly a wonderful man, for at sight of him three-fourths of my courage, and all my importance, oozed out at the heels of my boots.

"She will not see me. Very well," he replied, as if I had not spoken. And the simple words sounded like a sentence of death. "Then, M. Anne, I have a crow to pick with you. What compensation do you propose to make for the death of my servant? A decent, quiet fellow, whom you killed yesterday, poor man, because his enthusiasm for the true faith carried him away a little."

"Whom I killed because he drew a dagger on M. St. Croix de Caylus at the vicomte's gate," I answered, steadily. I had thought about this, of course, and was ready for it. "You are aware, M. de Bezers," I continued, "that the vicomte has jurisdiction extending to life and death over all persons within the valley?"

"My household excepted," he rejoined, quietly.

"Precisely; while they are within the curtilage of your house," I retorted. "However, as the punishment was summary, and the man had no time to confess himself, I am willing to —"

"Well?"

"To pay Father Pierre to say ten masses for his soul.''

The way the vidame received this surprised me. He broke into boisterous laughter. "By our Lady, my friend," he cried, with rough merriment, "but you are a joker! You are indeed. Masses! Why the man was a Protestant!"

And that startled me more than anything which had gone before; more indeed than I can explain. For it seemed to prove that this man, laughing his unholy laugh, was not like other men. He did not pick and choose his servants for their religion. He was sure that the Huguenot would stone his fellow at his bidding; the Catholic cry "Vive Coligny!" I was so completely taken aback that I found no words to answer him, and it was Croisette who said, smartly, "Then how about his enthusiasm for the true faith, M. le Vidame?"

"The true faith," he answered, "for my servants is my faith." Then a thought seemed to strike him. "What is more," he continued, slowly, "that it is the true and only faith for all, thousands will learn before the world is ten days older. Bear my words in mind, boy! They will come back to you. And now hear me," he went on in his usual tone. "I am anxious to accommodate a neighbor. It goes without saying that I would not think of putting you, M. Anne, to any trouble for the sake of that rascal of mine; but my people will expect something. Let the plaguey fellow who caused all this disturbance be given up to me, that I may hang him, and let us cry quits."

"That is impossible!" I answered, coolly. I had no need to ask what he meant. Give up Pavannes' messenger indeed! Never!

He regarded me — unmoved by my refusal — with a smile, under which I chafed, while I was impotent to resent it. "Do not build too much on a single blow, young gentleman," he said, shaking his head waggishly. "I had fought a dozen times when I was your age. However, I understand that you refuse to give me satisfaction?"

"In the mode you mention, certainly," I replied. "But —"

"Bah!" he exclaimed, with a sneer; "business first and pleasure afterward! Bezers will obtain satisfaction in his own way, I promise you that! And at his own time. And it will not be on

unfledged bantlings like you. But what is this
for?" And he rudely kicked the culverin, which
apparently he had not noticed before. "So! so!
understand," he continued, casting a sharp glance
at one and another of us. "You looked to be be-
sieged! Why, you booby, there is the shoot of
your kitchen midden, twenty feet above the roof
of old Fretis' store! And open, I will be sworn!
Do you think that I should have come this way
while there was a ladder in Caylus? Did you
take the wolf for a sheep?"

With that he turned on his heel, swaggering
away in the full enjoyment of his triumph, for
a triumph it was. We stood stunned, ashamed
to look one another in the face. Of course the
shoot was open. We remembered now that it
was, and we were so sorely mortified by his
knowledge and our folly that I failed in my
courtesy, and did not see him to the gate, as I
should have done. We paid for that later.

"He is the devil in person!" I exclaimed,
angrily, shaking my fist at the House of the Wolf,
as I strode up and down impatiently. "I hate
him worse!"

"So do I!" said Croisette, mildly. "But that
he hates us is a matter of more importance. At
any rate we will close the shoot."

"Wait a moment!" I replied, as after another
volley of complaints directed at our visitor, the

8

lad was moving off to see to it. What is going on down there?"

"Upon my word, I believe he is leaving us!" Croisette rejoined, sharply.

For there was a noise of hoofs below us, clattering on the pavement. Half a dozen horsemen were issuing from the House of the Wolf, the ring of their bridles and the sound of their careless voices coming up to us through the clear morning air. Bezers' valet, whom we knew by sight, was the last of them. He had a pair of great saddle-bags before him, and at sight of these we uttered a glad exclamation. "He is going!" I murmured, hardly able to believe my eyes. "He is going, after all!"

"Wait!" Croisette answered, dryly.

But I was right. We had not to wait long. He *was* going. In another moment he came out himself, riding a strong iron-gray horse, and we could see that he had holsters to his saddle. His steward was running beside him, to take, I suppose, his last orders. A cripple, whom the bustle had attracted from his usual haunt, the church porch, held up his hand for alms. The vidame, as he passed, cut him savagely across the face with his whip, and cursed him audibly.

"May the devil take him!" exclaimed Croisette in just rage. But I said nothing, remembering that the cripple was a particular pet of

Catherine's. I thought instead of an occasion, not so very long ago, when the vicomte being at home, we had had a great hawking party. Bezers and Catherine had ridden up the street together, and Catherine giving the cripple a piece of money, Bezers had flung to him all his share of the game. And my heart sank.

Only for a moment, however. The man was gone, or was going, at any rate. We stood silent and motionless, all watching, until, after what seemed a long interval, the little party of seven became visible on the white road far below us — to the northward, and moving in that direction. Still we watched them, muttering a word to one another, now and again, until presently the riders slackened their pace, and began to ascend the winding track that led to the hills and Cahors, and to Paris also, if one went far enough.

Then at length with a loud "Whoop!" we dashed across the terrace, Croisette leading, and so through the courtyard to the parlor, where we arrived breathless. "He is off!" Croisette cried, shrilly. "He has started for Paris! And bad luck go with him!" And we all flung up our caps and shouted.

But no answer, such as we expected, came from the women folk. When we picked up our caps and looked at Catherine, feeling rather foolish, she was staring at us with a white face and great scornful eyes. "Fools!" she said. "Fools!"

And that was all. But it was enough to take me aback. I had looked to see her face lighten at our news; instead it wore an expression I had never seen on it before. Catherine, so kind and gentle, calling us fools! And without cause! I did not understand it. I turned confusedly to Croisette. He was looking at her, and I saw that he was frightened. As for Madame Claude, she was crying in the corner. A presentiment of evil made my heart sink like lead. What had happened?

"Fools!" my cousin repeated with exceeding bitterness, her foot tapping the parquet unceasingly. "Do you think he would have stooped to avenge himself on *you?* On you! Or that he could hurt me one-hundredth part as much here —as—" She broke off stammering. Her scorn faltered for an instant. "Bah! he is a man! He knows!" she exclaimed, superbly, her chin in the air; "but you are boys. You do not understand!"

I looked amazedly at this angry woman. I had a difficulty in associating her with my cousin. As for Croisette, he stepped forward abruptly, and picked up a white object which was lying at her feet.

"Yes, read it!" she cried, "read it! Ah!" and she clinched her little hand, and in her passion struck the oak table beside her, so that a stain of blood sprang out of her knuckles. "Why did you not kill him? Why did you not do it when you had the chance? You were three to one," she hissed. "You had him in your power! You could have killed him, and you did not? Now he will kill me!"

Madame Claude muttered something tearfully; something about Pavannes and the saints. I looked over Croisette's shoulder, and read the letter. It began abruptly without any term of address, and ran thus: "I have a mission in Paris, mademoiselle, which admits of no delay, your mission as well as my own—to see Pavannes. You have won his heart. It is yours, and I will bring it you, or his right hand in token that he has yielded up his claim to yours. And to this I pledge myself."

The thing bore no signature. It was written in some red fluid—blood perhaps—a mean and sorry trick! On the outside was scrawled a direction to Mademoiselle de Caylus. And the packet was sealed with the vidame's crest, a wolf's head.

"The coward! the miserable coward!" Croisette cried. He was the first to read the meaning of the thing. And his eyes were full of tears—tears of rage.

For me, I was angry exceedingly. My veins

seemed full of fire, as I comprehended the mean
cruelty which could thus torture a girl.

"Who delivered this?" I thundered. "Who
gave it to mademoiselle? How did it reach her
hands? Speak, some of you!"

A maid, whimpering in the background, said
that Francis had given it to her to hand to
mademoiselle.

I ground my teeth together, while Marie, unbidden, left the room to seek Francis — and a stirrup
leather. The vidame had brought the note in his
pocket, no doubt, rightly expecting that he would
not get an audience of my cousin. Returning to
the gate alone he had seen his opportunity, and
given the note to Francis, probably with a small
fee to secure its transmission.

Croisette and I looked at one another, appre-
hending all this. "He will sleep at Cahors
to-night," I said, sullenly.

The lad shook his head and answered in a low
voice, "I am afraid not. His horses are fresh. I
think he will push on. He always travels
quickly. And now you know —"

I nodded, understanding only too well.

Catherine had flung herself into a chair. Her
arms lay nerveless on the table. Her face was
hidden in them. But now, overhearing us, or
stung by some fresh thought, she sprang to her
feet in anguish. Her face twitched, her form

seemed to stiffen as she drew herself up like one
in physical pain. "Oh, I can not bear it!" she
cried to us in dreadful tones. "Oh, will no one
do anything? I will go to him! I will tell him
I will give him up! I will do whatever he wishes
if he will only spare him!"

Croisette went from the room crying. It was a
dreadful sight for us — this girl in agony. And it
was impossible to reassure her! Not one of us
doubted the horrible meaning of the note, its
covert threat. Civil wars and religious hatred,
and I fancy Italian modes of thought, had for the
time changed our countrymen to beasts. Far
more dreadful things were done then than this
which Bezers threatened — even if he meant it
literally — far more dreadful things were suffered.
But in the fiendish ingenuity of his vengeance on
her, the helpless, loving woman, I thought Raoul
de Bezers stood alone. Alas! it fares ill with the
butterfly when the cat has struck it down. Ill
indeed!

Madame Claude rose and put her arms round
the girl, dismissing me by a gesture. I went
out, passing two or three scared servants, and
made at once for the terrace. I felt as if I
could only breathe there. I found Marie and St.
Croix together, silent, the marks of tears on their
faces. Our eyes met and they told one tale.

We all spoke at the same time. "When?"

we said. But the others looked to me for an answer.

I was somewhat sobered by that, and paused to consider before I replied. "At daybreak to-morrow," I decided presently. "It is an hour after noon already. We want money, and the horses are out. It will take an hour to bring them in. After that we might still reach Cahors to-night, perhaps; but more haste less speed, you know. No. At daybreak to-morrow we will start."

They nodded assent.

It was a great thing we meditated. No less than to go to Paris—the unknown city so far beyond the hills—and seek out M. de Pavannes, and warn him. It would be a race between the vidame and ourselves; a race for the life of Kit's suitor. Could we reach Paris first, or even within twenty-four hours of Bezers' arrival, we should in all probability be in time, and be able to put Pavannes on his guard. It had been the first thought of all of us to take such men as we could get together and fall upon Bezers wherever we found him, making it our simple object to kill him. But the lackeys M. le Vicomte had left with us, the times being peaceful and the neighbors friendly, were poor-spirited fellows. Bezers' handful, on the contrary, were reckless Swiss riders — like master, like men. We decided that it would be wiser simply to warn Pavannes, and then stand by him if necessary.

We might have dispatched a messenger. But our servants — Gil excepted, and he was too old to bear the journey — were ignorant of Paris. Nor could any one of them be trusted with a mission so delicate. We thought of Pavannes' courier indeed. But he was a Rochellois, and a stranger to the capital. There was nothing for it but to go ourselves.

Yet we did not determine on this adventure with light hearts, I remember. Paris loomed big and awesome in the eyes of all of us. The glamor of the court rather frightened than allured us. We felt that shrinking from contact with the world which a country life engenders, as well as that dread of seeming unlike other people which is peculiar to youth. It was a great plunge, and a dangerous one, which we meditated. And we trembled. If we had known more, especially of the future, we should have trembled more.

But we were young, and with our fears mingled a delicious excitement. We were going on an adventure of knight-errantry in which we might win our spurs. We were going to see the world and play men's parts in it; to save a friend and make our mistress happy!

We gave our orders, but we said nothing to Catherine or Madame Claude, merely bidding Gil tell them after our departure. We arranged for the immediate dispatch of a message to the vicomte at Bayonne, and charged Gil until he should hear from him to keep the gates closed, and look well to the shoot of the kitchen midden. Then, when all was ready, we went to our pallets, but it was with hearts throbbing with excitement and wakeful eyes.

"Anne! Anne!" said Croisette, rising on his elbow and speaking to me some three hours later, "what do you think the vidame meant this morning when he said that about the ten days?"

"What about the ten days?" I asked, peevishly. He had roused me just when I was at last falling asleep.

"About the world seeing that his was the true faith — in ten days?"

"I am sure I do not know. For goodness' sake let us go to sleep," I replied, for I had no patience with Croisette, talking such nonsense, when we had our own business to think about.

CHAPTER III.

THE sun had not yet risen above the hills when we three with a single servant behind us drew rein at the end of the valley, and easing our horses on the ascent, turned in the saddle to take a last look at Caylus—at the huddled gray town and the towers above it. A little thoughtful we all were, I think. The times were rough and our errand was serious. But youth and early morning are fine dispellers of care, and once on the uplands we trotted gaily forward, now passing through wide glades in the sparse oak forest, where the trees all leaned one way, now over bare, wide-swept downs, or once and again descending into a chalky bottom, where the stream bubbled through deep beds of fern, and a lonely farmhouse nestled amid orchards.

Four hours' riding, and we saw below us Cahors, filling the bend of the river. We cantered over the Vallandre Bridge, which there crosses the Lot, and so to my uncle's house of call in the square. Here we ordered breakfast, and announced with pride that we were going to Paris.

Our host raised his hands. "Now there!" he exclaimed, regret in his voice. "And if you had

arrived yesterday you could have traveled up
with the Vidame de Bezers! And you a small
party — saving your lordships' presence — and the
roads but so-so!"

"But the vidame was riding with only half a
dozen attendants also!" I answered, flicking my
boot in a careless way.

The landlord shook his head. "Ah, M. le
Vidame knows the world!" he answered, shrewdly.
"He is not to be taken off his guard, not he!
One of his men whispered me that twenty stanch
fellows would join him at Chateauroux. They
say the wars are over, but"—and the good man,
shrugging his shoulders, cast an expressive glance
at some fine flitches of bacon which were hanging
in his chimney. "However, your lordships know
better than I do," he added, briskly. "I am a
poor man. I only wish to live at peace with my
neighbors, whether they go to mass or sermon."

This was a sentiment so common in those days
and so heartily echoed by most men of substance,
both in town and country, that we did not stay to
assent to it; but having received from the worthy
fellow a token which would insure our obtaining
fresh cattle at Limoges, we took to the road again,
refreshed in body and with some food for thought.

Five-and-twenty attendants were more than
even such a man as Bezers, who had many enemies, traveled with in those days, unless accom-

panied by ladies. That the vidame had pro-
vided such a reinforcement seemed to point to a
wider scheme than the one with which we had
credited him. But we could not guess what his
plans were, since he must have ordered his people
before he heard of Catherine's engagement.
Either his jealousy therefore had put him on the
alert earlier, or his threatened attack on Pavannes
was only a part of a larger plot. In either case
our errand seemed more urgent, but scarcely more
hopeful.

The varied sights and sounds, however, of the
road—many of them new to us—kept us from
dwelling overmuch on this. Our eyes were young,
and whether it was a pretty girl lingering behind a
troop of gipsies, or a pair of strollers from Valencia
—*jongleurs* they still called themselves — singing
in the old dialect of Provence, or a Norman
horse-dealer with his string of cattle tied head and
tail, or the Puy de Dome to the eastward over
the Auvergne hills, or a tattered old soldier
wounded in the wars—fighting for either side,
according as their lordships inclined — we were
pleased with all.

Yet we never forgot our errand. We never, I
think, rose in the morning—too often stiff and
sore — without thinking, "To-day, or to-morrow,
or the next day," as the case might be, "we
shall make all right for Kit!" For Kit! Perhaps

it was the purest enthusiasm we were ever to feel, the least selfish aim we were ever to pursue. For Kit!

Meanwhile we met few travelers of rank on the road. Half the nobility of France were still in Paris enjoying the festivities which were being held to mark the royal marriage. We obtained horses where we needed them without difficulty. And though we had heard much of the dangers of the way, infested as it was said to be by disbanded troopers, we were not once stopped or annoyed.

But it is not my intention to chronicle all the events of this my first journey, though I dwell on them with pleasure; or to say what I thought of the towns, all new and strange to me, through which we passed. Enough that we went by way of Limoges, Chateauroux, and Orleans, and that at Chateauroux we learned the failure of one hope we had formed. We had thought that Bezers when joined there by his troopers would not be able to get relays; and that on this account we might, by traveling post, overtake him; and possibly slip by him between that place and Paris. But we learned at Chateauroux that his troop had received fresh orders to go to Orleans and await him there, the result being that he was able to push forward with relays so far. He was evidently in hot haste. For leaving there with his horses fresh he passed through Angerville, forty miles short of Paris, at noon, whereas we reached it on the evening of the same day — the sixth after leaving Caylus.

We rode into the yard of the inn — a large place, seeming larger in the dusk — so tired that we could scarcely slip from our saddles. Jean, our servant, took the four horses, and led them across to the stables, the poor beasts hanging their heads, and following meekly. We stood a moment stamping our feet and stretching our legs. The place seemed in a bustle, the clatter of pans and dishes proceeding from the windows over the entrance, with a glow of light and the sound of feet hurrying in the passages. There were men too, half a dozen or so standing at the doors of the stables, while others leaned from the windows. One or two lanterns just kindled glimmered here and there in the semi-darkness, and in a corner two smiths were shoeing a horse.

We were turning from all this to go in, when we heard Jean's voice raised in altercation, and thinking our rustic servant had fallen into trouble, we walked across to the stables near which he and the horses were still lingering. "Well, what is it?" I said, sharply.

"They say that there is no room for the horses," Jean answered querulously, scratching his head, half-sullen, half-cowed, a country servant all over.

"And there is not!" cried the foremost of the gang about the door, hastening to confront us in turn. His tone was insolent, and it needed but half an eye to see that his fellows were inclined to back him up. He stuck his arms akimbo and faced us with an impudent smile. A lantern on the ground beside him throwing an uncertain light on the group, I saw that they all wore the same badge.

"Come," I said, sternly, "the stables are large, and your horses can not fill them. Some room must be found for mine."

"To be sure! Make way for the king!" he retorted. While one jeered "*Vive le roi!*" and the rest laughed. Not good-humoredly, but with a touch of spitefulness.

Quarrels between gentlemen's servants were as common then as they are to-day. But the masters seldom condescended to interfere. "Let the fellows fight it out," was the general sentiment. Here, however, poor Jean was overmatched, and we had no choice but to see to it ourselves.

"Come, men, have a care that you do not get into trouble," I urged, restraining Croisette by a touch, for I by no means wished to have a repetition of the catastrophe which had happened at Caylus. "These horses belong to the Vicomte de Caylus. If your master be a friend of his, as may very probably be the case, you will run the risk of getting into trouble."

I thought I heard, as I stopped speaking, a subdued muttering, and fancied I caught the words, "*Papegot!* Down with the Guises!" But the spokesman's only answer aloud was "Cock-a-doodle-doo!" "Cock-a-doodle-doo!" he repeated, flapping his arms in defiance. "Here is a cock of a fine hackle!" And so on, and so forth, while he turned grinning to his companions, looking for their applause.

I was itching to chastise him, and yet hesitating, lest the thing should have its serious side, when a new actor appeared. "Shame, you brutes!" cried a shrill voice above us — in the clouds it seemed. I looked up and saw two girls, coarse and handsome, standing at a window over the stable, a light between them. "For shame! Don't you see that they are mere children? Let them be," cried one.

The men laughed louder than ever; and for me, I could not stand by and be called a child. "Come here," I said, beckoning to the man in the doorway. "Come here, you rascal, and I will give you the thrashing you deserve for speaking to a gentleman!"

He lounged forward, a heavy fellow, taller than myself and six inches wider at the shoulders. My heart failed me a little as I measured him. But the thing had to be done. If I was slight, 1 was wiry as a hound, and in the excite-

4

ment had forgotten my fatigue. I snatched from Marie a loaded riding-whip he carried, and stepped forward.

"Have a care, little man!" cried the girl, gaily — yet half in pity, I think; "or that fat pig will kill you!"

My antagonist did not join in the laugh this time. Indeed it struck me that his eye wandered, and that he was not so ready to enter the ring as his mates were to form it. But before I could try his mettle a hand was laid on my shoulder. A man appearing from I do not know where — from the dark fringe of the group, I suppose — pushed me aside, roughly, but not discourteously.

"Leave this to me!" he said, coolly stepping before me. "Do not dirty your hands with the knave, master. I am pining for work, and the job will just suit me! I will fit him for the worms before the nuns above can say an *Ave!*"

I looked at the newcomer. He was a stout fellow; not over-tall, nor over-big; swarthy, with prominent features. The plume of his bonnet was broken, but he wore it in a rakish fashion, and altogether he swaggered with so dare-devil an air, clinking his spurs and swinging out his long sword recklessly, that it was no wonder three or four of the nearest fellows gave back a foot.

"Come on!" he cried, boisterously, forming a ring by the simple process of sweeping his blade

from side to side, while he made the dagger in his
left hand flash round his head. "Who is for the
game? Who will strike a blow for the little
admiral? Will you come one, two, three at once,
or all together? Anyway, come on, you—"
And he closed his challenge with a volley of
frightful oaths, directed at the group opposite.

"It is no quarrel of yours," said the big man,
sulkily, making no show of drawing his sword,
but rather drawing back himself.

"All quarrels are my quarrels, and no quarrels
are your quarrels. That is about the truth, I
fancy!" was the smart retort, which our cham-
pion rendered more emphatic by a playful lunge
that caused the big bully to skip again.

There was a loud laugh at this, even among the
enemy's backers. "Bah, the great pig!" ejaculated the girl above. "Spit him!" and she spat
down on the whilom Hector, who made no great
figure now.

"Shall I bring you a slice of ham, my dear?"
asked my rakehelly friend, looking up and
making his sword play round the shrinking
wretch. "Just a titbit, my love?" he added
persuasively. "A mouthful of white liver and
caper sauce?"

"Not for me, the beast!" the girl cried, amid
the laughter of the yard.

"Not a bit? If I warrant him tender? Ladies'
meat?"

"Bah! no!" and she stolidly spat down again.

"Do you hear? The lady has no taste for you," the tormentor cried. "Pig of a Gascon!" And deftly sheathing his dagger, he seized the big coward by the ear, and turning him round, gave him a heavy kick which sent him spinning over a bucket, and down against the wall. There the bully remained, swearing and rubbing himself by turns, while the victor cried boastfully, "Enough of him. If any one wants to take up his quarrel, Blaise Buré is his man. If not, let us have an end of it. Let some one find stalls for the gentleman's horses before they catch a chill, and have done with it. As for me," he added, and then he turned to us and removed his hat with an exaggerated flourish, "I am your lordships' servant to command."

I thanked him with a heartiness half-earnest, half-assumed. His cloak was ragged, his trunk hose, which had once been fine enough, were stained and almost pointless. He swaggered inimitably, and had led-captain written large upon him. But he had done us a service, for Jean had no further trouble about the horses. And besides one has a natural liking for a brave man, and this man was brave beyond question.

"You are from Orleans," he said, respectfully enough, but as one asserting a fact, not asking a question.

"Yes," I answered, somewhat astonished. "Did you see us come in?"

"No, but I looked at your boots, gentlemen," he replied. "White dust, north; red dust, south. Do you see?"

"Yes, I see," I said, with admiration. "You must have been brought up in a sharp school, M. Buré."

"Sharp masters make sharp scholars," he replied, grinning. And that answer I had occasion to remember afterward.

"You are from Orleans, also?" I asked, as we prepared to go in.

"Yes, from Orleans, too, gentlemen; but earlier in the day. With letters — letters of importance!" And bestowing something like a wink of confidence on us, he drew himself up, looked sternly at the stable-folk, patted himself twice on the chest, and finally twirled his moustache, and smirked at the girl above, who was chewing straws.

I thought it likely enough that we might find it hard to get rid of him, but this was not so. After listening with gratification to our repeated thanks, he bowed with the same grotesque flourish, and marched off as grave as a Spaniard, humming:

" Ce petit homme tant joli!
Qui toujours cause et toujours rit,
Qui toujours baise sa mignonne,
Dieu gard' de mal ce petit homme!"

On our going in, the landlord met us politely, but with curiosity, and a simmering of excitement also in his manner. "From Paris, my lords?" he asked, rubbing his hands and bowing low, "or from the south?"

"From the south," I answered. "From Orleans, and hungry and tired, Master Host."

"Ah!" he replied, disregarding the latter part of my answer, while his little eyes twinkled with satisfaction. "Then I dare swear, my lords, you have not heard the news?" He halted in the narrow passage, and lifting the candle he carried, scanned our faces closely, as if he wished to learn something about us before he spoke.

"News!" I answered, brusquely, being both tired, and as I had told him, hungry. "We have heard none, and the best you can give us will be that our supper is ready to be served."

But even this snub did not check his eagerness to tell his news. "The Admiral de Coligny," he said, breathlessly, "you have not heard what has happened to him?"

"To the admiral? No, what?" I inquired rapidly. I was interested at last.

For a moment let me digress. The few of my age will remember, and the many younger will have been told, that at this time the Italian queen-mother was the ruling power in France. It was **Catherine de' Medici's** first object to maintain

her influence over Charles the IX., her son,
who, rickety, weak, and passionate, was already
doomed to an early grave. Her second, to support the royal power by balancing the extreme
Catholics against the Huguenots. For the latter
purpose she would coquet first with one party,
then with the other. At the present moment she
had committed herself more deeply than was her
wont to the Huguenots. Their leaders, the
Admiral Gaspard de Coligny, the King of
Navarre, and the Prince of Condé, were supposed to be high in favor, while the chiefs of the
other party, the Duke of Guise, and the two
Cardinals of his house, the Cardinal of Lorraine
and the Cardinal of Guise, were in disgrace;
which, as it seemed, even their friend at court,
the queen's favorite son, Henry of Anjou, was
unable to overcome.

Such was the outward aspect of things in
August, 1572, but there was not wanting rumors
that already Coligny, taking advantage of the
footing given him, had gained an influence over
the young king which threatened Catherine de'
Medici herself. The admiral, therefore, to whom
the Huguenot half of France had long looked to
as its leader was now the object of the closest
interest to all, the Guise faction hating him,
as the alleged assassin of the Duke of Guise,
with an intensity which probably was not to be

found in the affection of his friends, popular with
the latter as he was.

Still, many who were not Huguenots had a
regard for him as a great Frenchman and a gallant
soldier.   We — though we were of the old faith,
and the other side — had heard much of him, and
much good.   The vicomte had spoken of him
always as a great man, a man mistaken, but brave,
honest, and capable in his error. Therefore it was
that when the landlord mentioned him, I forgot
even my hunger.

"He was shot, my lords, as he passed through
the Rue des Fosses, yesterday," the man declared
with bated breath.   "It is not known whether he
will live or die.   Paris is in an uproar, and there
are some who fear the worst."

"But," I said, doubtfully, "who has dared to
do this? He had a safe conduct from the king
himself."

Our host did not answer; shrugging his
shoulders instead, he opened the door and
ushered us into the eating-room.

Some preparations for our meal had already
been made at one end of the long board.   At the
other was seated a man past middle age, richly
but simply dressed.   His gray hair, cut short
about a massive head, and his grave, resolute face,
square-jawed and deeply-lined, marked him as
one to whom respect was due apart from his

clothes. We bowed to him as we took our seats.

He acknowledged the salute, fixing us a moment with a penetrating glance, and then resumed his meal. I noticed that his sword and belt were propped against a chair at his elbow, and a dag, apparently loaded, lay close to his hand by the candlestick. Two lackeys waited behind his chair, wearing the badge we had remarked in the inn yard.

We began to talk, speaking in low tones that we might not disturb him. The attack on Coligny had, if true, its bearing on our own business. For if a Huguenot so great and famous and enjoying the king's special favor still went in Paris in danger of his life, what must be the risk that such an one as Pavannes ran? We had hoped to find the city quiet. If instead it should be in a state of turmoil Bezers' chances were so much the better; and ours — and Kit's, poor Kit's — so much the worse.

Our companion had by this time finished his supper. But he still sat at the table, and seemed to be regarding us with some curiosity. At length he spoke. "Are you going to Paris, young gentlemen?" he asked, his tone harsh and high-pitched.

We answered in the affirmative.

"To-morrow?" he questioned.

"Yes," we answered, and expected him to continue the conversation. But instead he became silent, gazing abstractedly at the table; and what with our meal and our own talk, we had almost forgotten him again, when looking up, I found him at my elbow, holding out in silence a small piece of paper.

I started, his face was so grave. But seeing that there were half a dozen guests of a meaner sort at another table close by, I guessed that he merely wished to make a private communication to us; and hastened to take the paper and read it. It contained a scrawl of four words only:

"Va chasser l'Idole."

No more. I looked at him puzzled, able to make nothing out of it. St. Croix wrinkled his brow over it with the same result. It was no good handing it to Marie, therefore.

"You do not understand?" the stranger continued, as he put the scrap of paper back in his pouch.

"No," I answered, shaking my head. We had all risen out of respect to him, and were standing a little group about him.

"Just so; it is all right then," he answered, looking at us as it seemed to me with grave good-nature. "It is nothing. Go your way. But I have a son yonder, not much younger than you, young gentlemen. And if you had understood, I should have said to you, 'Do not go! There are enough sheep for the shearer.' "

He was turning away with this oracular saying when Croisette touched his sleeve. "Pray can you tell us if it be true," the lad said, eagerly, "that the Admiral de Coligny was wounded yesterday?"

"It is true," the other answered, turning his grave eyes on his questioner, while for a moment his stern look failed him. "It is true, my boy," he added with an air of strange solemnity. "Whom the Lord loveth, he chasteneth. And, God forgive me for saying it, whom he would destroy he first maketh mad."

He had gazed with peculiar favor at Croisette's girlish face, I thought; Marie and I were dark and ugly by the side of the boy. But he turned from him now with a queer, excited gesture, thumping his gold-headed cane on the floor. He called his servants in a loud, rasping voice, and left the room in seeming anger, driving them before him, the one carrying his bag, and the other, two candles.

When I came down early next morning the first person I met was Blaise Buré. He looked rather fiercer and more shabby by daylight than candlelight. But he saluted me respectfully, and this, since it was clear that he did not respect many people, inclined me to regard him with

favor. It is always so, the more savage the dog
the more highly we prize its attentions. I asked
him who the Huguenot noble was who had supped
with us, for a Huguenot we knew he must be.

"The Baron de Rosny," he answered, adding
with a sneer, "He is a careful man! If they were
all like him, with eyes on both sides of his head
and a dag by his candle — well, my lord, there
would be one more king in France, or one less!
But they are a blind lot, as blind as bats." He
muttered something further in which I caught the
word "to-night." But I did not hear it all, or
understand any of it.

"Your lordships are going to Paris?" he
resumed, in a different tone. When I said that
we were, he looked at me in a shamefaced way,
half-timid, half-arrogant. "I have a small favor
to ask of you then," he said. "I am going to
Paris myself. I am not afraid of odds, as you
have seen. But the roads will be in a queer state
if there be anything on foot in the city, and —
well, I would rather ride with you gentlemen than
alone."

"You are welcome to join us," I said. "But
we start in half an hour. Do you know Paris
well?" "As well as my sword-hilt," he replied,
briskly, relieved, I thought, by my acquiescence;
"and I have known that from my breeching. If
you want a game at *paume*, or a pretty girl to

kiss, I can put you in the way for the one or the other."

The half-rustic shrinking from the great city which I felt, suggested to me that our swash-buckling friend might help us if he would. "Do you know M. de Pavannes?" I asked, impulsively. "Where he lives in Paris, I mean?"

"M. Louis de Pavannes?" quoth he.

"Yes."

"I know," he replied, slowly, rubbing his chin and looking at the ground in thought, "where he had his lodgings in town a while ago, before— Ah! I do know! I remember," he added, slapping his thigh, "when I was in Paris a fortnight ago I was told that his steward had taken lodgings for him in the Rue St. Antoine."

"Good!" I answered, overjoyed. "Then we want to dismount there, if you can guide us straight to the house."

"I can," he replied, simply. "And you will not be the worse for my company. Paris is a queer place when there is trouble to the fore, but your lordships have got the right man to pilot you through it."

I did not ask him what trouble he meant, but ran indoors to buckle on my sword and tell Marie and Croisette of the ally I had secured. They were much pleased, as was natural, so that

we took the road in excellent spirits, intending
to reach the city in the afternoon. But Marie's
horse cast a shoe, and it was some time before we
could find a smith. Then at Etampes, where we
stopped to lunch, we were kept an unconscion-
able time waiting for it. And so we approached
Paris for the first time at sunset. A ruddy glow
was at the moment warming the eastern heights,
and picking out with flame the twin towers of
Notre Dame, and the one tall tower of St.
Jacques la Boucherie. A dozen roofs higher
than their neighbors shone hotly, and a great
bank of cloud, which lay north and south, and
looked like a man's hand stretched over the city,
changed gradually from blood-red to violet, and
from violet to black, as evening fell.

Passing within the gates and across first one
bridge and then another, we were astonished and
utterly confused by the noise and hubbub
through which we rode. Hundreds seemed to be
moving this way and that in the narrow streets.
Women screamed to one another from window to
window. The bells of half a dozen churches rang
the curfew. Our country ears were deafened.
Still our eyes had leisure to take in the tall
houses, with their high-pitched roofs, and here
and there a tower built into the wall; the quaint
churches, and the groups of townsfolk — sullen
fellows some of them, with a fierce gleam in their

eyes — who, standing in the mouths of reeking alleys, watched us go by.

But presently we had to stop. A crowd had gathered to watch a little cavalcade of six gentlemen pass across our path. They were riding two and two, lounging in their saddles and chattering to one another, disdainfully unconscious of the people about them, or the remarks they excited. Their graceful bearing and the richness of their dress and equipment surpassed anything I had ever seen. A dozen pages and lackeys were attending them on foot, and the sound of their jests and laughter came to us over the heads of the crowd.

While I was gazing at them, some movement of the throng drove back Buré's horse against mine. Buré himself uttered a savage oath, uncalled for, so far as I could see. But my attention was arrested the next moment by Croisette, who tapped my arm with his riding whip. "Look!" he cried in some excitement, "is not that he?"

I followed the direction of the lad's finger — as well as I could for the plunging of my horse which Buré's had frightened — and scrutinized the last pair of the troop. They were crossing the street in which we stood, and I had only a side view of them, or rather of the nearer rider. He was a singularly handsome man, in age about twenty-two or twenty-three, with long lovelocks

falling on his lace collar and cloak of orange silk.
His face was sweet and kindly, and gracious to a
marvel. But he was a stranger to me.

"I could have sworn," exclaimed Croisette,
"that that was Louis himself — M. de Pavannes!"

"That?" I answered, as we began to move
again, the crowd melting before us. " Oh, dear,
no!"

"No! no! The farther man!" he explained.

But I had not been able to get a good look at
the farther of the two. We turned in our saddles
and peered after him. His back in the dusk
certainly reminded me of Louis. Buré, however,
who said he knew M. de Pavannes by sight,
laughed at the idea. "Your friend," he said, "is
a wider man than that!" And I thought he was
right there — but then it might be the cut of the
clothes. "They have been at the Louvre playing
paume, I'll be sworn!" he went on. "So the
admiral must be better. The one next us was
M. de Teligny, the admiral's son-in-law. And
the other, whom you mean, was the Comte de
la Rochefoucault."

We turned, as he spoke, into a narrow street
near the river, and could see not far from us a mass
of dark buildings, which Buré told us was the
Louvre, the king's residence. Out of this street
we turned into a short one, and here Buré drew
rein and rapped loudly at some heavy gates. It

was so dark that when, these being opened, he led
the way into a courtyard, we could see little more
than a tall, sharp-gabled house, projecting over us
against a pale sky, and a group of men and
horses in one corner. Buré spoke to one of the
men, and begging us to dismount, said the foot-
man would show us to M. de Pavannes.

The thought that we were at the end of our
long journey, and in time to warn Louis of his
danger, made us forget all our exertions, our
fatigue and stiffness. Gladly throwing the bridles
to Jean, we ran up the steps after the servant.
The thing was done. Hurrah! the thing was
done!

The house — as we passed through a long passage and up some steps — seemed full of people.
We heard voices and the ring of arms more than
once. But our guide, without pausing, led us to
a small room lighted by a hanging lamp. "I
will inform M. de Pavannes of your arrival," he
said, respectfully, and passed behind a curtain,
which seemed to hide the door of an inner apart-
ment. As he did so the clink of glasses and the
hum of conversation reached us.

"He has company supping with him," I said
nervously. I tried to flip some of the dust from
my boots with my whip. I remembered that this
was Paris.

"He will be surprised to see us," quoth Croi-

sette, laughing—a little shyly, too, I think.
And so we stood waiting.

I began to wonder as minutes passed by—the
gay company we had seen putting it in my mind,
I suppose—whether M. de Pavannes of Paris
might not turn out to be a very different person
from Louis de Pavannes of Caylus; whether the
king's courtier would be as friendly as Kit's
lover. And I was still thinking of this without
having settled the point to my satisfaction, when
the curtain was thrust aside again. A very tall
man, wearing a splendid suit of black and silver
and a stiff trencher-like ruff, came quickly in and
stood smiling at us, a little dog in his arms. The
little dog sat up and snarled, and Croisette
gasped. It was not our old friend Louis certainly! It was not Louis de Pavannes at all. It
was no old friend at all. It was the Vidame de
Bezers!

"Welcome, gentlemen!" he said, smiling at us
—and never had the cast been so apparent in his
eyes. "Welcome to Paris, M. Anne!"

CHAPTER IV.

ENTRAPPED!

THERE was a long silence. We stood glaring at
him, and he smiled upon us -- as a cat smiles.
Croisette told me afterward that he could have
died of mortification — of shame and anger that we
had been so outwitted. For myself I did not at
once grasp the position. I did not understand.
I could not disentangle myself in a moment from
the belief in which I had entered the house — that
it was Louis de Pavannes' house. But I seemed
vaguely to suspect that Bezers had swept him
aside and taken his place. My first impulse
therefore — obeyed on the instant — was to stride
to the vidame's side and grasp his arm. "What
have you done?" I cried, my voice sounding
hoarsely, even in my own ears. "What have you
done with M. de Pavannes? Answer me!"

He showed just a little more of his sharp white
teeth, as he looked down at my face — a flushed
and troubled face doubtless. "Nothing — yet,"
he replied very mildly. And he shook me off.

"Then," I retorted, "how do you come here?"

He glanced at Croisette and shrugged his
shoulders, as if I had been a spoiled child. "M.
Anne does not seem to understand," he said, with

mock courtesy, that I have the honor to welcome
him to my house, the Hotel Bezers, Rue de
Platrière."

"The Hotel Bezers! Rue de Platrière!" I
cried, confusedly. "But Blaise Buré told us that
this was the Rue St. Antoine!"

"Ah!" he replied, as if slowly enlightened,
the hypocrite! "Ah! I see!" and he smiled
grimly. "So you have made the acquaintance of
Blaise Buré, my excellent master of the horse!
Worthy Blaise! Indeed, indeed; now I understand. And you thought, you whelps," he
continued, and as he spoke his tone changed
strangely, and he fixed us suddenly with angry
eyes, "to play a rubber with me! With me, you
imbeciles! You thought the wolf of Bezers could
be hunted down like any hare! Then listen, and
I will tell you the end of it. You are now in my
house and absolutely at my mercy. I have two-
score men within call who would cut the throats
of three babes at the breast, if I bade them!
Ay," he added, a wicked exultation shining in
his eyes, "they would, and like the job!"

He was going on to say more, but I interrupted
him. The rage I felt, caused as much by the
thought of our folly as by his arrogance, would
let me be silent no longer. "First, M. de Bezers,
first," I broke out fiercely, my words leaping over
one another in my haste, "a word with you! Let

me tell you what I think of you! You are a
treacherous hound, vidame! A cur! a beast! and
I spit upon you! Traitor and assassin!" I
shouted, "is that not enough? Will nothing
provoke you? If you call yourself a gentleman,
draw!"

He shook his head; he was still smiling, still
unmoved. "I do not do my own dirty work,"
he said, quietly, "nor stint my footmen of their
sport, boy."

"Very well!" I retorted. And with the words
I drew my sword, and sprang as quick as lightning to the curtain by which he had entered.
"Very well, we will kill you first!" I cried
wrathfully, my eye on his eye, and every savage
passion in my breast aroused, "and take our
chance with the lackeys afterward! Marie!
Croisette!" I cried, shrilly, "on him, lads!"

But they did not answer! They did not move
or draw. For the moment indeed the man was in
my power. My wrist was raised, and I had my
point at his breast. I could have run him through
by a single thrust. And I hated him. Oh, how
I hated him! But he did not stir. Had he
spoken, had he moved so much as an eyelid, or
drawn back his foot, or laid his hand on his hilt,
I should have killed him there. But he did not
stir and I could not do it. My hand dropped.
"Cowards!" I cried, glancing bitterly from him

to them—they had never failed me before. "Cowards!" I muttered, seeming to shrink into myself as I said the word. And I flung my sword clattering on the floor.

"That is better!" he drawled, quite unmoved, as if nothing more than words had passed, as if he had not been in peril at all. "It was what I was going to ask you to do. If the other young gentlemen will follow your example, I shall be obliged. Thank you. Thank you."

Croisette, and a minute later Marie, obeyed him to the letter! I could not understand it. I folded my arms and gave up the game in despair, and but for very shame I could have put my hands to my face and cried. He stood in the middle under the lamp, a head taller than the tallest of us, our master. And we stood round him trapped, beaten, for all the world like children. Oh, I could have cried! This was the end of our long ride, our aspirations, our knight-errantry!

"Now perhaps you will listen to me," he went on smoothly, "and hear what I am going to do. I shall keep you here, young gentlemen, until you can serve me by carrying to mademoiselle, your cousin, some news of her betrothed. Oh, I shall not detain you long," he added, with an evil smile. "You have arrived in Paris at a fortunate moment. There is going to be a—well, there is a little scheme on foot appointed for to-night—

singularly lucky you are!—for removing some
objectionable people, some friends of ours perhaps
among them, M. Anne. That is all. You will
hear shots, cries, perhaps screams. Take no
notice. You will be in no danger. For M. de
Pavannes," he continued, his voice sinking, "I
think that by morning I shall be able to give you
a—a more particular account of him to take to
Caylus—to mademoiselle, you understand."

For a moment the mask was off. His face took
a somber brightness. He moistened his lips with
his tongue as though he saw his vengeance worked
out then and there before him, and was gloating
over the picture. The idea that this was so took
such a hold upon me that I shrank back, shuddering, reading too in Croisette's face the same
thought—and a late repentance. Nay, the malig-
nity of Bezers' tone, the savage gleam of joy in
his eyes, appalled me to such an extent that I
fancied for a moment I saw in him the devil
incarnate.

He recovered his composure very quickly, however, and turned carelessly toward the door.
"If you will follow me," he said, "I will see you
disposed of. You may have to complain of your
lodging—I have other things to think of to-night
than hospitality. But you shall not need to complain of your supper.

He drew aside the curtain as he spoke, and

passed into the next room before us, not giving a thought apparently to the possibility that we might strike him from behind. There certainly was an odd quality apparent in him at times which seemed to contradict what we knew of him.

The room we entered was rather long than wide, hung with tapestry, and lighted by silver lamps Rich plate, embossed, I afterward learned, by Cellini the Florentine — who died that year, I remember — and richer glass from Venice, with a crowd of meaner vessels filled with meats and drinks, covered the table, disordered as by the attacks of a numerous party. But save a servant or two by the distant dresser, and an ecclesiastic at the far end of the table, the room was empty.

The priest rose as we entered, the vidame saluting him as if they had not met that day. "You are welcome, M. le Coadjuteur," he said, saying it coldly, however, I thought. And the two eyed one another with little favor; rather as birds of prey about to quarrel over the spoil than as host and guest. Perhaps the coadjutor's glittering eyes and great beak-like nose made me think of this.

"Ho! ho!" he said, looking piercingly at us, and no doubt we must have seemed a miserable and dejected crew enough. "Who are these? Not the first fruits of the night, eh?"

The vidame looked darkly at him. "No," he

answered, brusquely. "They are not. I am not particular out of doors, Coadjutor, as you know, but this is my house, and we are going to supper. Perhaps you do not comprehend the distinction. Still it exists — for me," with a sneer.

This was as good as Greek to us. But I so shrank from the priest's malignant eyes, which would not quit us, and felt so much disgust mingled with my anger that when Bezers by a gesture invited me to sit down, I drew back. "I will not eat with you," I said, sullenly, speaking out of a kind of dull obstinacy, or perhaps a childish petulance.

It did not occur to me that this would pierce the vidame's armor. Yet a dull red showed for an instant in his cheek, and he eyed me with a look that was not all ferocity, though the veins in his great temples swelled. A moment, nevertheless, and he was himself again. "Armand," he said quietly to the servant, "these gentlemen will not sup with me. Lay for them at the other end."

Men are odd. The moment he gave way to me I repented of my words. It was almost with reluctance that I followed the servant to the lower part of the table. More than this, mingled with the hatred I felt for the vidame, there was now a strange sentiment toward him, almost of admiration, that had its birth, I think, in the moment when I held his life in my hand and he had not flinched.

We ate in silence; even after Croisette, by grasping my hand under the table, had begged me not to judge him hastily. The two at the upper end talked fast, and from the little that reached us I judged that the priest was pressing some course on his host, which the latter declined to take.

Once Bezers raised his voice. "I have my own ends to serve!" he broke out angrily, adding a fierce oath which the priest did not rebuke, "and I shall serve them. But there I stop. You have your own. Well, serve them, but do not talk to me of the cause! The cause! To hell with the cause! I have my cause, and you have yours, and my lord of Guise has his! And you will not make me believe that there is any other!"

"The king's?" suggested the priest, smiling sourly.

"Say rather the Italian woman's," the vidame answered recklessly, meaning the queen-mother, Catherine de' Medici, I supposed.

"Well, then, the cause of the church?" the priest persisted.

"Bah! The church? It is you, my friend!" Bezers rejoined, rudely tapping his companion — at that moment in the act of crossing himself — on the chest. "The church?" he continued.

"No, no, my friend. I will tell you what you are doing. You want me to help you to get rid of your branch, and you offer in return to aid me with mine, and then, say you, there will be no stick left to beat either of us. But you may understand once for all "— and the vidame struck his hand heavily down among the glasses —"that I will have no interference with my work, master Clerk! None! Do you hear? And as for yours, it is no business of mine. That is plain speaking, is it not?"

The priest's hand shook as he raised a full glass to his lips, but he made no rejoinder, and the vidame, seeing we had finished, rose. "Armand!" he cried, his face still dark, "take these gentlemen to their chamber. You understand!"

We stiffly acknowledged his salute—the priest taking no notice of us—and followed the servant from the room, going along a corridor and up a steep flight of stairs, and seeing enough by the way to be sure that resistance was hopeless. Doors opened silently as we passed, and grim fellows, in corselets and padded coats, peered out. The clank of arms and murmur of voices sounded continuously about us; and as we passed a window the jingle of bits, and the hollow clang of a restless hoof on the flags below, told us that the great house was for the time a fortress. I wondered much. For this was Paris, a city with gates and guards; the night a short August night. Yet the loneliest manor in Quercy could scarcely have bristled with more pikes and musquetoons on a winter's night and in time of war.

No doubt these signs impressed us all, and Croisette not least. For suddenly I heard him stop, as he followed us up the narrow staircase, and begin without warning to stumble down again as fast as he could. I did not know what he was about; but muttering something to Marie, I followed the lad to see. At the foot of the flight of stairs I looked back. Marie and the servant were standing in suspense, where I had left them. I heard the latter bid us angrily to return.

But by this time Croisette was at the end of the corridor; and reassuring the fellow by a gesture I hurried on, until brought to a standstill by a man opening a door in my face. He had heard our returning footsteps, and eyed me suspiciously, but gave way after a moment with a grunt of doubt. I hastened on, reaching the door of the room in which we had supped in time to see something which filled me with grim astonishment, so much so that I stood rooted where I was, too proud at any rate to interfere.

Bezers was standing, the leering priest at his elbow, and Croisette was stooping forward, his hands stretched out in an attitude of supplication.

"Nay, but M. le Vidame," the lad cried, as I stood, the door in my hand, "it were better to stab her at once than break her heart! Have pity on *her!* If you kill him, you kill her!"

The vidame was silent, seeming to glower on the boy. The priest sneered. "Hearts are soon mended, especially women's," he said.

"But not Kit's!" Croisette said, passionately, otherwise ignoring him. "Not Kit's! You do not know her, vidame! Indeed you do not!"

The remark was ill-timed. I saw a spasm of anger distort Bezers' face. "Get up, boy!" he snarled, "I wrote to mademoiselle what I would do, and that I shall do! A Bezers keeps his word. By the God above us — if there be a God, and in the devil's name I doubt it to-night! — I shall keep mine! Go!"

His great face was full of rage. He looked over Croisette's head as he spoke, as if appealing to the Great Registrar of his vow, in the very moment in which he all but denied him. I turned and stole back the way I had come, and heard Croisette follow.

That little scene completed my misery. After that I seemed to take no heed of anything or anybody until I was aroused by the grating of our jailer's key in the lock, and became aware that he was gone, and that we were alone in a small room under the tiles. He had left the candle on the floor, and we three stood round it. Save for the long shadows we cast on the walls and two pallets hastily thrown down in one corner, the place was empty. I did not look much at it, and I would not look at the others. I flung myself on one of the pallets and turned my face to the wall, despairing. I thought bitterly of the failure we had made of it, and of the vidame's triumph. I cursed St. Croix especially for that last touch of humiliation he had set to it. Then forgetting myself as my anger abated, I thought of Kit so far away at Caylus — of Kit's pale, gentle face, and her sorrow. And little by little I forgave Croisette. After all he had not begged for us — he had not stooped for our sakes, but for hers.

I do not know how long I lay at see-saw between these two moods. Or whether during that time the others talked or were silent, moved about the room or lay still. But it was Croisette's hand on my shoulder, touching me with a quivering eagerness that instantly communicated itself to my limbs, which recalled me to the room and its shadows. "Anne!" he cried. "Anne! Are you awake?"

"What is it?" I asked, sitting up and looking at him.

"Marie," he began, "has —"

But there was no need for him to finish. I saw

that Marie was standing at the far side of the room by the unglazed window, which, being in a sloping part of the roof, inclined slightly also. He had raised the shutter which closed it, and on his tip-toes — for the sill was almost his own height from the floor — was peering out. I looked sharply at Croisette. "Is there a gutter outside?" I whispered, beginning to tingle all over as the thought of escape for the first time occurred to me.

"No," he answered in the same tone. "But Marie says he can see a beam below, which he thinks we can reach."

I sprang up, promptly displaced Marie, and looked out. When my eyes grew accustomed to the gloom I discerned a dark chaos of roofs and gables stretching as far as I could see before me. Nearer, immediately under the window, yawned a chasm, a narrow street. Beyond this was a house rather lower than that in which we were, the top of its roof not quite reaching the level of my eyes. "I see no beam," I said.

"Look below!" quoth Marie, stolidly.

I did so, and then saw that fifteen or sixteen feet below our window there was a narrow beam which ran from our house to the opposite one, for the support of both, as is common in towns. In the shadow near the far end of this — it was so directly under our window that I could only see the other end of it—I made out a casement, faintly illuminated from within.

I shook my head.

"We can not get down to it," I said, measuring the distance to the beam and the depth below it, and shivering.

"Marie says we can, with a short rope," Croisette replied. His eyes were glistening with excitement.

"But we have no rope!" I retorted. I was dull, as usual. Marie made no answer. Surely he was the most stolid and silent of brothers. I turned to him. He was taking off his waistcoat and neckerchief.

"Good!" I cried. I began to see now. Off came our scarfs and kerchiefs also, and fortunately they were of home make, long and strong. And Marie had a hank of four-ply yarn in his pocket, as it turned out, and I had some stout new garters, and two or three yards of thin cord, which I had brought to mend the girths, if need should arise. In five minutes we had fastened them cunningly together.

"I am the l ghtest," said Croisette.

"But Marie has the steadiest head," I objected. We had learned that long ago — that Marie could walk the coping-stones of the battlements with as little concern as we paced a plank set on the ground.

"True," Croisette had to admit. "But he must come last, because whoever does so will have to let himself down."

I had not thought of that, and I nodded. It seemed that the lead was passing out of my hands and I might resign myself. Still one thing I would have. As Marie was ·to come last, I would go first. My weight would best test the rope. And accordingly it was so decided.

There was no time to be lost. At any moment we might be interrupted. So the plan was no sooner conceived than carried out. The rope was made fast to my left wrist. Then I mounted on Marie's shoulders, and climbed — not without quavering — through the window, taking as little time over it as possible, for a bell was already proclaiming midnight.

All this I had done on the spur of the moment. But outside, hanging by my hands in the darkness, the strokes of the great bell in my ears, I had a moment in which to think. The sense of the vibrating depth below me, the airiness, the space and gloom around, frightened me. "Are you ready?" muttered Marie, perhaps with a little impatience. He had not a scrap of imagination, had Marie.

"No! wait a minute!" I blurted out, clinging to the sill, and taking a last look at the bare room and the two dark figures between me and

the light. "No!" I added, hurriedly. "Croisette — boys, I called you cowards just now. I
take it back. I did not mean it. That is all, " I
gasped. " Let go!"

A warm touch on my hand. Something like a
sob.

The next moment I felt myself sliding down
the face of the house, down into the depth. The
light shot up. My head turned giddily. I clung,
oh, how I clung to that rope! Half-way down
the thought struck me that in case of accident
those above might not be strong enough to pull
me up again. But it was too late to think of
that, and in another second my feet touched the
beam. I breathed again. Softly, very gingerly,
I made good my footing on the slender bridge,
and, disengaging the rope, let it go. Then, not
without another qualm, I sat down astride of the
beam and whistled in token of success. Success
so far!

It was a strange position, and I have often
dreamed of it since. In the darkness about me
Paris lay to all seemingly asleep. A veil, and
not the veil of night only, was stretched between
it and me; between me, a mere lad, and the
strange secrets of a great city; stranger, grimmer,
more deadly that night than ever before or since.
How many men were watching under those dim-
ly-seen roofs, with arms in their hands? How

many sat with murder at heart? How many
were waking, who at dawn would sleep forever,
or sleeping, who would wake only at the knife's
edge? These things I could not know, any more
than I could picture how many boon companions
were parting at that instant, just risen from the
dice, one to go blindly — the other watching him
— to his death? I could not imagine, thank
heaven for it, these secrets, or a hundredth part
of the treachery and cruelty and greed that
lurked at my feet, ready to burst all bounds at a
pistol-shot. It had no significance for me that
the past day was the 23d of August, or that the
morrow was St. Bartholomew's feast?

No. Yet mingled with the jubilation which
the possibility of triumph over our enemy raised
in my breast, there was certainly a foreboding.
The vidame's hints, no less than his open boasts,
had pointed to something to happen before morning — something wider than the mere murder of
a single man. The warning also which the Baron
de Rosny had given us at the inn occurred to me
with new meaning. And I could not shake the
feeling off. I fancied, as I sat in the darkness
astride of my beam, that I could see, closing the
narrow vista of the street, the heavy mass of the
Louvre; and that the murmur of voices and the
tramp of men assembling came from its courts,
with now and again the stealthy challenge of a

sentry, the restrained voice of an officer. Scarcely a wayfarer passed beneath me; so few, indeed, that I had no fear of being detected from below. And yet, unless I was mistaken, a furtive step, a subdued whisper, were borne to me on every breeze, from every quarter. And the night was full of phantoms.

Perhaps all this was mere nervousness, the outcome of my position. At any rate I felt no more of it when Croisette joined me. We had our daggers, and that gave me some comfort. If we could once gain entrance to the house opposite, we had only to beg, or in the last resort, force our way downstairs and out, and then to hasten with what speed we might to Pavannes' dwelling. Clearly it was a question of time only now, whether Bezers' band or we should first reach it. And struck by this I whispered Marie to be quick. He seemed to be long in coming.

He scrambled down hand over hand at last, and then I saw that he had not lingered above for nothing. He had contrived, after getting out of the window, to let down the shutter. And more, he had at some risk lengthened our rope, and made a double line of it, so that it ran round a hinge of the shutter; and when he stood beside us, he took it by one end and disengaged it. Good, clever Marie!

"Bravo!" I said softly, clapping him on the

back. "Now they will not know which way the birds have flown!"

So there we all were, one of us, I confess, trembling. We slid easily enough along the beam to the opposite house. But once there in a row, one behind the other, with our faces to the wall, and the night air blowing slantwise—well I am nervous on a height and I gasped. The window was a good six feet above the beam. The casement—it was unglazed—was open, veiled by a thin curtain, and alas! protected by three horizontal bars—stout bars they looked.

Yet we were bound to get up, and to get in; and I was preparing to rise to my feet on the giddy bridge as gingerly as I could, when Marie crawled quickly over us, and swung himself up to the narrow sill, much as I should mount a horse on the level. He held out his foot to me, and making an effort I reached the same dizzy perch. Croisette for the time remained below.

A narrow window-ledge sixty feet above the pavement, and three bars to cling to! I cowered to my holdfasts, envying even Croisette. My legs dangled airily, and the black chasm of the street seemed to yawn for me. For a moment I turned sick. I recovered from that to feel desperate. I remembered that go forward we must, bars or no bars. We could not regain our old prison if we would.

It was equally clear that we could not go forward if the inmates should object. On that narrow perch even Marie was helpless. The bars of the window were close together. A woman, a child, could disengage our hands, and then — I turned sick again. I thought of the cruel stones. I glued my face to the bars, and pushing aside a corner of the curtain, looked in.

There was only one person in the room — a woman, who was moving about fully dressed, late as it was. The room was a mere attic, the counterpart of that we had left. A box-bed with a canopy roughly nailed over it stood in a corner. A couple of chairs were by the hearth, and all seemed to speak of poverty and bareness. Yet the woman whom we saw was richly dressed, though her silks and velvets were disordered. I saw a jewel gleam in her hair, and others on her hands. When she turned her face toward us — a wild, beautiful face, perplexed and tear-stained — I knew her instantly for a gentlewoman, and when she walked hastily to the door, and laid her hand upon it, and seemed to listen; when she shook the latch and dropped her hands in despair and went back to the hearth, I made another discovery. I knew at once, seeing her there, that we were likely but to change one prison for another. Was every house in Paris then a dungeon? And did each roof cover its tragedy?

"Madame," I said, speaking softly, to attract her attention. "Madame!"

She started violently, not knowing whence the sound came, and looked round, at the door first. Then she moved toward the window, and with an affrighted gesture drew the curtain rapidly aside.

Our eyes met. What if she screamed and aroused the house? What, indeed? "Madame," I said again, speaking hurriedly, and striving to reassure her by the softness of my voice, "we implore your help! Unless you assist us we are lost."

"You! Who are you?" she cried, glaring at us wildly, her hand to her head. And then she murmured to herself, "Mon Dieu! what will become of me?"

"We have been imprisoned in the house opposite," I hastened to explain, disjointedly I am afraid; "and we have escaped. We can not get back if we would. Unless you let us enter your room and give us shelter —"

"We shall be dashed to pieces on the pavement," supplied Marie, with perfect calmness — nay, with apparent enjoyment.

"Let you in here?" she answered, starting back in new terror. "It is impossible."

She reminded me of our cousin, being, like her, pale and dark-haired. She wore her hair in a coronet, disordered now. But though she was

still beautiful, she was older than Kit, and lacked
her pliant grace.   I saw all this, and judging her
nature, I spoke out of my despair.   "Madame," I
said, piteously, "we are only boys.   Croisette,
come up!"   Squeezing myself still more tightly
into my corner of the ledge, I made room for him
between us.   "See, madame," I cried, craftily,
"will you not have pity on three boys?"

St. Croix's boyish face and fair hair arrested
her attention, as I had expected.   Her expression
grew softer, and she murmured, "Poor boy!"

I caught at the opportunity.   "We do but seek
a passage through your room," I said, fervently.
Good heavens! what had we not at stake?   What
if she should remain obdurate?   "We are in
trouble, in despair," I panted.   "So, I believe,
are you.   We will help you, if you will first save
us.   We are boys, but we can fight for you."

"Whom am I to trust?" she exclaimed, with a
shudder.   "But, heaven forbid," she continued,
her eyes on Croisette's face, "that, wanting help,
I should refuse to give it.   Come in, if you will."

I poured out my thanks, and had forced my
head between the bars—at imminent risk of its
remaining there—before the words were well out
of her mouth.   But to enter was no easy task
after all.   Croisette did, indeed, squeeze through
at last, and then by force pulled first one and
then the other of us after him.   But only necessity and that chasm behind could have nerved us,

I think, to go through a process so painful.
When I stood, at length on the floor, I seemed to
be one great abrasion from head to foot. And
before a lady, too!

But what a joy I felt, nevertheless. A fig for
Bezers now. He had called us boys, and we were
boys; but he should yet find that we could
thwart him. It could be scarcely half an hour
after midnight; we might still be in time. I
stretched myself and trod the level floor jubi-
lantly, and then noticed, while doing so, that our
hostess had retreated to the door and was eyeing
us timidly, half-scared.

I advanced to her with my lowest bow, sadly
missing my sword. "Madame," I said, "I am
M. Anne de Caylus, and these are my brothers.
And we are at your service."

"And I," she replied, smiling faintly — I do not
know why—"am Madame de Pavannes. I grate-
fully accept your offers of service."

"De Pavannes!" I exclaimed, amazed and overjoyed. Madame de Pavannes! Why, she must
be Louis' kinswoman! No doubt she could tell
us where he was lodged, and so rid our task of
half its difficulty. Could anything have fallen
out more happily? "You know, then, M. Louis
de Pavannes?" I continued, eagerly.

"Certainly," she answered, smiling with a rare,
shy sweetness this time. "Very well indeed.
He is my husband."

CHAPTER V.

A PRIEST AND A WOMAN.

"HE is my husband!"

The statement was made in the purest innocence; yet never, as may well be imagined, did
words fall with more stunning force. Not one of
us answered or, I believe, moved so much as a
limb or an eyelid. We only stared, wanting time
to take in the astonishing meaning of the words,
and then more time to think what they meant to
us in particular.

Louis de Pavannes' wife! Louis de Pavannes
married! If the statement were true — and we
could not doubt, looking in her face, that at least
she thought she was telling the truth — it meant
that we had been fooled indeed! That we had
had this journey for nothing, and run this risk
for a villain. It meant that the Louis de Pavannes who had won our boyish admiration was the
meanest, the vilest of court-gallants; that Mademoiselle de Caylus had been his sport and play-
thing; and that we in trying to be beforehand
with Bezers had been striving to save a scoundrel
from his due. It meant all that, as soon as we
grasped it in the least.

"Madame," said Croisette, gravely, after a

pause so prolonged that her smile faded pitifully from her face, scared by our strange looks, "your husband has been some time away from you? He only returned, I think, a week or two ago?"

"That is so," she answered, naively, and our last hope vanished. "But what of that? He was back with me again, and only yesterday — only yesterday!" she continued, clasping her hands, "we were so happy."

"And now, madame?"

She looked at me, not comprehending.

"I mean," I hastened to explain, "we do not understand how you come to be here. And a prisoner." I was really thinking that her story might throw some light upon ours.

"I do not know, myself," she said. "Yesterday, in the afternoon, I paid a visit to the abbess of the Ursulines."

"Pardon me," Croisette interposed quickly, "but are you not of the new faith? A Huguenot?"

"Oh, yes," she answered, eagerly. "But the abbess is a very dear friend of mine, and no bigot. Oh, nothing of that kind, I assure you. When I am in Paris I visit her once a week. Yesterday, when I left her, she begged me to call here and deliver a message."

"Then," I said, "you know this house?'

"Very well, indeed," she replied. "It is the sign of the 'Hand and Glove,' one door out of the Rue Platrière. I have been in Master Mirepoix's shop more than once before. I came here yesterday to deliver the message, leaving my maid in the street, and I was asked to come upstairs, and still up until I reached this room. Asked to wait a moment, I began to think it strange that I should be brought to so wretched a place, when I had merely a message for Mirepoix's ear about some gauntlets. I tried the door; I found it locked. Then I was terrified, and made a noise."

We all nodded. We were busy building up theories — or it might be one and the same theory — to explain this. "Yes," I said, eagerly.

"Mirepoix came to me then. 'What does this mean?' I demanded. He looked ashamed of himself, but he barred my way. 'Only this,' he said, at last, 'that your ladyship must remain here a few hours — two days at most. No harm whatever is intended to you. My wife will wait upon you, and, when you leave us, all shall be explained.' He would say no more, and it was in vain I asked him if he did not take me for some one else; if he thought I was mad. To all he answered, 'No.' And when I dared him to detain me, he threatened force. Then I succumbed. I have been here since, suspecting I know not what, but fearing everything."

"That is ended, madame," I answered, my hand on my breast, my soul in arms for her. Here, unless I was mistaken, was one more unhappy and more deeply wronged even than Kit; one, too, who owed her misery to the same villain. "Were there nine glovers on the stairs," I declared, roundly, "we would take you out and take you home! Where are your husband's apartments?"

"In the Rue de Saint Merri, close to the church. We have a house there."

"M. de Pavannes," I suggested, cunningly, "is doubtless distracted by your disappearance."

"Oh, surely," she answered, with earnest simplicity, while the tears sprang to her eyes. Her innocence — she had not the germ of a suspicion — made me grind my teeth with wrath. Oh, the base wretch! The miserable rascal! What did the women see, I wondered — what had we all seen in this man, this Pavannes, that won for him our hearts, when he had only a stone to give in return?

I drew Croisette and Marie aside, apparently to consider how we might force the door. "What is the meaning of this?" I said softly, glancing at the unfortunate lady. "What do you think, Croisette?"

I knew well what the answer would be.

"Think!" he cried, with fiery impatience,

"What can any one think except that that villain Pavannes has himself planned his wife's abduction? Of course it is so! His wife out of the way he is free to follow up his intrigues at Caylus. He may then marry Kit or— curse him!"

"No," I said, sternly, "cursing is no good. We must do something more. And yet—we have promised Kit, you see, that we would save him— we must keep our word. We must save him from Bezers at least."

Marie groaned.

But Croisette took up the thought with ardor. "From Bezers?" he cried, his face aglow. "Ay, true! So we must! But then we will draw lots who shall fight him and kill him."

I extinguished him by a look. "We shall fight him in turn," I said, "until one of us kill him. There you are right. But your turn comes last. Lots indeed! We have no need of lots to learn which is the eldest."

I was turning from him—having very properly crushed him—to look for something which we could use to force the door, when he held up his hand to arrest my attention. We listened, looking at one another. Through the window came unmistakable sounds of voices. "They have discovered our flight," I said, my heart sinking.

Luckily we had had the forethought to draw the curtain across the casement. Bezers' people could therefore, from their window, see no more than ours, dimly lighted and indistinct. Yet they would no doubt guess the way we had escaped, and hasten to cut off our retreat below. For a moment I looked at the door of our room, half-minded to attack it and fight our way out, taking the chance of reaching the street before Bezers' folk should have recovered from their surprise and gone down. But then I looked at madame. How could we insure her safety in the struggle? While I hesitated the choice was taken from us. We heard voices in the house below, and heavy feet on the stairs.

We were between two fires. I glanced irreso-lutely round the bare garret, with its sloping roof, searching for a better weapon. I had only my dagger. But in vain. I saw nothing that would serve. "What will you do?" Madame de Pavannes murmured, standing pale and trem-bling by the hearth, and looking from one to another. Croisette plucked my sleeve before I could answer, and pointed to the box-bed with its scanty curtains. "If they see us in the room," he urged softly, "while they are half in and half out, they will give the alarm. Let us hide our-selves yonder. When they are inside — you understand?"

He laid his hand on his dagger. The muscles of the lad's face grew tense. I did understand him. "Madame," I said, quickly, "you will not betray us?"

She shook her head. The color returned to her cheeks and the brightness to her eyes. She was a true woman. The sense that she was protecting others deprived her of fear for herself.

The footsteps were on the topmost stair now, and a key was thrust with a rasping sound into the lock. But before it could be turned — it fortunately fitted ill — we three had jumped on the bed and were crouching in a row at the head of it, where the curtains of the alcove concealed, and only just concealed, us from any one standing at the end of the room near the door.

I was the outermost, and through a chink could see what passed. One, two, three people came in, and the door was closed behind them. Three people, and one of them a woman! My heart, which had been in my mouth, returned to its place, for the vidame was not one. I breathed freely; only I dared not communicate my relief to the others, lest my voice should be heard. The first to come in was the woman closely cloaked and hooded. Madame de Pavannes cast on her a single doubtful glance, and then to my astonishment threw herself into her arms, mingling her sobs with little joyous cries of "Oh, Diane! Oh, Diane!"

"My poor little one!" the newcomer exclaimed,

soothing her with tender touches on hair and
shoulder. "You are safe now! Quite safe!"

"You have come to take me away?"

"Of course we have!" Diane answered cheerfully, still caressing her. "We have come to take
you to your husband. He has been searching
for you everywhere. He is distracted with grief,
little one."

"Poor Louis!" ejaculated the wife.

"Poor Louis, indeed!" the rescuer answered.
"But you will see him soon. We only learned at
midnight where you were. You have to thank
M. le Coadjuteur here for that. He brought me
the news, and at once escorted me here to fetch
you."

"And to restore one sister to another," said the
priest silkily, as he advanced a step. He was the
very same priest whom I had seen two hours
before with Bezers, and had so greatly disliked.
I hated his pale face as much now as I had then.
Even the errand of good on which he had come
could not blind me to his thin-lipped mouth, to
his mock humility and crafty eyes. "I have had
no task so pleasant for many days," added he,
with every appearance of a desire to propitiate.

But, seemingly, Madame de Pavannes had something of the same feeling toward him which I had
myself, for she started at the sound of his voice,
and disengaging herself from her sister's arms —

7

it seemed it was her sister — shrank back from
the pair. She bowed indeed in acknowledgment
of his words. But there was little gratitude in
the movement, and less warmth. I saw the sister's face — a brilliantly beautiful face it was —
brighter eyes and lips and more lovely auburn
hair I have never seen — even Kit would have
been plain and dowdy beside her — I saw it
harden strangely. A moment before, the two had
been in one another's arms. Now they stood
apart, somehow chilled and disillusioned. The
shadow of the priest had fallen upon them — had
come between them.

At this crisis the fourth person present asserted
himself. Hitherto he had stood silent just within
the door; a plain man, plainly dressed, somewhat
over sixty and gray-haired. He looked discon-
certed and embarrassed, and I took him for
Mirepoix — rightly, as it turned out.

"I am sure," he now exclaimed, his voice
trembling with anxiety, or it might be with fear,
"your ladyship will regret leaving here. You
will indeed. No harm would have happened to
you. Madame d'O does not know what she is
doing, or she would not take you away. She
does not know what she is doing!" he repeated,
earnestly.

"Madame d'O!" cried the beautiful Diane, her
brown eyes darting fire at the unlucky culprit, her

voice full of angry disdain, "How dare you—such as you—mention my name? Wretch!".

She flung the last word at him, and the priest took it up. "Ay, wretch! Wretched man indeed!" he repeated slowly, stretching out his long thin hand and laying it like the claw of some bird of prey on the tradesman's shoulder, which flinched, I saw, under the touch. "How dare you—such as you—meddle with matters of the nobility? Matters that do not concern you? Trouble! I see trouble hanging over this house, Mirepoix! Much trouble!"

The miserable fellow trembled visibly under the covert threat. His face grew pale. His lips quivered. He seemed fascinated by the priest's gaze. "I am a faithful son of the church," he muttered; but his voice shook so that the words were scarcely audible. "I am known to be such! None better known in Paris, M. le Coadjuteur."

"Men are known by their works!" the priest retorted. "Now, now," he continued, abruptly raising his voice, and lifting his hand in a kind of exaltation, real or feigned, "is the appointed time! And now is the day of salvation! And woe, Mirepoix, woe! woe! to the backslider, and to him that putteth his hand to the plow and looketh back to-night!"

The layman cowered and shrank before his fierce denunciation; while Madame de Pavannes gazed from one to the other as if her dislike for the priest was so great, that seeing the two thus quarreling, she almost forgave Mirepoix his offense. "Mirepoix said he could explain," she murmured, irresolutely.

The coadjutor fixed his baleful eyes on him. "Mirepoix," he said, grimly, "can explain nothing! Nothing! I dare him to explain!"

And certainly Mirepoix thus challenged was silent. "Come," the priest continued peremptorily, turning to the lady who had entered with him, "your sister must leave with us at once. We have no time to lose."

"But what — what does it mean?" Madame de Pavannes said, as though she hesitated even now. "Is there danger still?"

"Danger!" the priest exclaimed, his form seeming to swell, and the exaltation I had before read in his voice and manner again asserting itself. "I put myself at your service, madame, and danger disappears. I am as God to-night, with powers of life and death! You do not understand me? Presently you shall. But you are ready. We will go then. Out of the way, fellow!" he thundered, advancing upon the door.

But Mirepoix, who had placed himself with his back to it, to my astonishment did not give way. His full bourgeois face was pale; yet peeping through my chink, I read in it a desperate reso-

lution. And oddly — very oddly, because I knew
that in keeping Madame de Pavannes a prisoner
he must be in the wrong — I sympathized with
him. Low-bred trader, tool of Pavannes though
he was, I sympathized with him, when he said
firmly:

"She shall not go!"

"I say she shall!" the priest shrieked, losing
all control over himself. "Fool! Madman! You
know not what you do!" As the words passed
his lips he made an adroit forward movement,
surprised the other, clutched him by the arms,
and with a strength I should never have thought
lay in his meagre frame, flung him some paces
into the room. "Fool!" he hissed, shaking his
crooked fingers at him in malignant triumph.
"There is no man in Paris, do you hear — or
woman either — shall thwart me to-night!"

"Is that so? Indeed?"

The words and the cold, cynical voice were not
those of Mirepoix; they came from behind. The
priest wheeled round as if he had been stabbed in
the back. I clutched Croisette, and arrested the
cramped limb I was moving under cover of the
noise. The speaker was Bezers! He stood in the
open doorway, his great form filling it from post
to post, the old gibing smile on his face. We
had been so taken up, actors and audience alike,
with the altercation, that no one had heard him

ascend the stairs. He still wore the black and silver suit, but it was half-hidden now under a dark riding cloak which just disclosed the glitter of his weapons. He was booted and spurred and gloved as for a journey.

"Is that so?" he repeated, mockingly, as his gaze rested in turn on each of the four, and then traveled sharply round the room. "So you will not be thwarted by any man in Paris to-night, eh? Have you considered, my dear coadjutor, what a large number of people there are in Paris? It would amuse me very greatly now —and I'm sure it would the ladies, too, who must pardon my abrupt entrance — to see you put to the test; pitted against — shall we say the Duke of Anjou? Or Monsieur de Guise, our great man? Or the admiral? Say the admiral, foot to foot?"

Rage and fear — rage at the intrusion, fear of the intruder — struggled in the priest's face. "How do you come here, and what do you want?" he inquired, hoarsely. If looks and tones could kill, we three, trembling behind our flimsy screen, had been freed at that moment from our enemy.

"I have come in search of the young birds whose necks you were for stretching, my friend!" was Bezers' answer. "They have vanished. Birds they must be, for unless they have come into this house by that window, they have flown away with wings."

"They have not passed this way," the priest declared, stoutly, eager only to get rid of the other—and I blessed him for the words. "I have been here since I left you."

But the vidame was not one to accept any man's statement. "Thank you; I think I will see for myself," he answered, coolly. "Madame," he continued, speaking to Madame de Pavannes, as he passed her, "permit me."

He did not look at her, or see her emotion, or I think he must have divined our presence. And happily the others did not suspect her of knowing more than they did. He crossed the floor at his leisure, and sauntered to the window, watched by them with impatience. He drew aside the curtain, and tried each of the bars, and peered through the opening both up and down. An oath and an expression of wonder escaped him. The bars were standing, and firm and strong; and it did not occur to him that we could have passed between them. I am afraid to say how few inches they were apart.

As he turned, he cast a casual glance at the bed —at us, and hesitated. He had the candle in his hand, having taken it to the window the better to examine the bars, and it obscured his sight. He did not see us. The three crouching forms, the strained white faces, the staring eyes, that lurked in the shadow of the curtain escaped him. The

wild beating of our hearts did not reach his ears.
And it was well for him that it was so. If he
had come up to the bed I think that we should
have killed him; I know that we should have tried.
All the blood in me had gone to my head, and I
saw him through a haze — larger than life. The
exact spot near the buckle of his cloak where I
would strike him, downward and inward, an
inch above the collar-bone — this only I saw
clearly. I could not have missed it. But he
turned away, his face darkening, and went back
to the group near the door, and never knew the
risk he had run.

CHAPTER VI.

MADAME'S FRIGHT.

AND we breathed again. The agony of suspense which Bezers' pause had created passed away. But the night already seemed to us as a week of nights; an age of experience, an æon of adventures cut us off — as we lay shaking behind the curtain — from Caylus and its life. Paris had proved itself more treacherous than we had even expected to find it. Everything and everyone shifted, and wore one face one minute and one another. We had come to save Pavannes' life at the risk of our own; we found him to be a villain! Here was Mirepoix owning himself a treacherous wretch, a conspirator against a woman; we sympathized with him. The priest had come upon a work of charity and rescue; we loathed the sound of his voice, and shrank from him, we knew not why, seeming only to read a dark secret, a gloomy threat in each doubtful word he uttered. He was the strangest enigma of all. Why did we fear him? Why did Madame de Pavannes, who apparently had known him before, shudder at the touch of his hand? Why did his shadow come, even between her and her sister, and estrange them, so that from the moment Pavannes' wife

(105)

saw him standing by Diane's side, she forgot that the latter had come to save, and looked on her in doubt and sorrow, almost with repugnance.

We left the vidame going back to the fireplace. He stooped to set down the candle by the hearth. "They are not here," he said, as he straightened himself again, and looked curiously at his companions. He had apparently been too much taken up with the pursuit to notice them before. "That is certain, so I have the less time to lose," he continued. "But I would—yes, my dear coadjutor, I certainly would like to know before I go, what you are doing here? Mirepoix— Mirepoix is an honest man. I did not expect to find you in *his* house. And two ladies? Two! Fie, Coadjutor. Ha! Madame d'O, is it? My dear lady," he continued, addressing her in a whimsical tone," do not start at the sound of your own name! It would take a hundred hoods to hide your eyes, or bleach your lips to the common color. I should have known you at once had I looked at you. And your companion? Phew!"

He broke off, whistling softly. It was clear that he recognized Madame de Pavannes, and recognized her with astonishment. The bed creaked as I craned my neck to see what would follow. Even the priest seemed to think that some explanation was necessary, for he did not wait to be questioned.

"Madame de Pavannes," he said in a dry, husky voice, and without looking up, "was spirited hither yesterday, and detained against her will by this good man, who will have to answer for it. Madame d'O discovered her where-abouts, and asked me to escort her here without loss of time, to enforce her sister's release."

"And her restoration to her distracted hus-band?"

"Just so," the priest assented, acquiring con-fidence, I thought.

"And madame desires to go?"

"Surely! Why not?"

"Well," the vidame drawled, his manner such as to bring the blood to Madame de Pavannes' cheek, "it depends on the person who — to use your phrase, M. le Coadjuteur — spirited her hither."

"And that," madame herself retorted, raising her head, while her voice quivered with indig-nation and anger, "was the Abbess of the Ursu-lines. Your suspicions are base, worthy of you and unworthy of me, M. le Vidame! Diane!" she continued, sharply, taking her sister's arm, and casting a disdainful glance at Bezers, "let us go. I want to be with my husband. I am stifled in this room."

"We are going, little one," Diane murmured, reassuringly. But I noticed that the speaker's

animation, which had been as a soul to her beauty
when she entered the room, was gone. A strange
stillness — was it fear of the vidame? — had taken
its place.

"The Abbess of the Ursulines?" Bezers continued, thoughtfully. "*She* brought you here,
did she?" There was surprise, genuine surprise,
in his voice. "A good soul, and, I think I have
heard, a friend of yours. Umph!"

"A very dear friend," madame answered, stiffly.
"Now, Diane!"

"A dear friend! And she spirited you hither
yesterday!" commented the vidame, with the air
of one solving an anagram. "And Mirepoix
detained you; respectable Mirepoix, who is said
to have a well-filled stocking under his pallet,
and stands well with the bourgeois. He is in
the plot. Then at a very late hour, your affec-
tionate sister, and my good friend the coadjutor,
enter to save you. From what?"

No one spoke. The priest looked down, his
cheek livid with anger.

"From what?" Bezers continued, with grim
playfulness. "There is the mystery. From the
clutches of this profligate Mirepoix, I suppose.
From the dangerous Mirepoix. Upon my honor,"
with a sudden ring of resolution in his tone, "I
think you are safer here; I think you had better
stay where you are, madame, until morning!
And risk Mirepoix!"

"Oh, no! no!" Madame cried, vehemently.

"Oh, yes! yes!" he replied. "What do you say, Coadjutor? Do you not think so?"

The priest looked down sullenly. His voice shook as he murmured in answer, "Madame will please herself. She has a character, M. le Vidame. But if she prefer to stay here — well!"

"Oh, she has a character, has she?" rejoined the giant, his eyes twinkling with evil mirth, "and she should go home with you, and my old friend Madame d'O, to save it! That is it, is it? No, no," he continued when he had had his silent laugh out, "Madame de Pavannes will do very well here — very well here until morning. We have work to do. Come. Let us go and do it."

"Do you mean it?" said the priest, starting and looking up with a subtle challenge — almost a threat — in his tone.

"Yes, I do."

Their eyes met, and seeing their looks, I chuckled, nudging Croisette. No fear of their discovering us now. I recalled the old proverb which says that when thieves fall out, honest men come by their own, and speculated on the chance of the priest freeing us once for all from M. de Bezers.

But the two were ill-matched. The vidame could have taken up the other with one hand and dashed his head on the floor. And it did not end

there.   I doubt if in craft the priest was his equal.
Behind a frank brutality Bezers — unless his
reputation belied him — concealed an Italian intel-
lect.   Under a cynical recklessness he veiled a
rare cunning and a constant suspicion; enjoying
in that respect a combination of apparently
opposite qualities, which I have known no other
man to possess in an equal degree, unless it might
be his late majesty, Henry the Great.   A child
would have suspected the priest; a veteran might
have been taken in by the vidame.

And indeed the priest's eyes presently sank.
"Our bargain is to go for nothing?" he muttered,
sullenly.

"I know of no bargain," quoth the vidame.
"And I have no time to lose, splitting hairs here.
Set it down to what you like.   Say it is a whim
of mine, a fad, a caprice.   Only understand that
Madame de Pavannes stays.   We go.   And —" he
added this, as a sudden thought seemed to strike
him, "though I would not willingly use compul-
sion to a lady, I think Madame d'O had better
come, too."

"You speak masterfully," the priest said with
a sneer, forgetting the tone he had himself used a
few minutes before to Mirepoix.

"Just so.   I have forty horsemen over the way,"
was the dry answer.   "For the moment, I am
master of the legions, Coadjutor."

"That is true," Madame d'O said, so softly that I started. She had scarcely spoken since Bezers' entrance. As she spoke now, she shook back the hood from her face and disclosed the chestnut hair clinging about her temples—deep blots of color on the abnormal whiteness of her skin. "That is true, M. de Bezers," she said. "You have the legions; you have the power. But you will not use it, I think, against an old friend. You will not do us this hurt when I—But listen."

He would not. In the very middle of her appeal he cut her short—brute that he was! "No madame!" he burst out violently, disregarding the beautiful face, the supplicating glance, that might have moved a stone, "that is just what I will not do. I will not listen! We know one another. Is not that enough?"

She looked at him fixedly. He returned her gaze, not smiling now, but eyeing her with a curious watchfulness.

And after a long pause she turned from him. "Very well," she said, softly, and drew a deep, quivering breath, the sound of which reached us. "Then let us go." And without—strangest thing of all—bestowing a word or look on her sister, who was weeping bitterly in a chair, she turned to the door and led the way out, a shrug of her shoulders the last thing I marked.

The poor lady heard her departing step, however, and sprang up. It dawned upon her that she was being deserted. "Diane! Diane!" she cried, distractedly—and I had to put my hand on Croisette to keep him quiet, there was such fear and pain in her tone —"I will go! I will not be left behind in this dreadful place! Do you hear? Come back to me, Diane!"

It made my blood run wildly. But Diane did not come back. Strange! And Bezers too was unmoved. He stood between the poor woman and the door, and by a gesture bid Mirepoix and the priest pass out before him. "Madame," he said — and his voice, stern and hard as ever, expressed no jot of compassion for her, rather such an impatient contempt as a puling child might elicit —"you are safe here. And here you will stop! Weep if you please," he added, cynically, "you will have fewer tears to shed to-morrow."

His last words — they certainly were odd ones — arrested her attention. She checked her sobs, being frightened, I think, and looked up at him. Perhaps he had spoken with this in view, for while she still stood at gaze, her hands pressed to her bosom, he slipped quickly out and closed the door behind him. I heard a muttering for an instant outside, and then the tramp of feet descending the stairs. They were gone, and we were still undiscovered.

For madame, she had clean forgotten our

presence—of that I am sure—and the chance of
escape we might afford. On finding herself alone
she gazed a short time in alarmed silence at the
door, and then ran to the window and peered out,
still trembling, terrified, silent. So she remained
a while.

She had not noticed that Bezers on going out
had omitted to lock the door behind him. I had.
But I was unwilling to move hastily. Some one
might return to see to it before the vidame left the
house. And besides the door was not over
strong, and if locked would be no obstacle to the
three of us when we had only Mirepoix to deal
with. So I kept the others where they were by a
nudge and a pinch, and held my breath a moment,
straining my ears to catch the closing of the door
below. I did not hear that. But I did catch a
sound that otherwise might have escaped me, but
which now riveted my eyes to the door of our
room. Some one, in the silence which followed the
trampling on the stairs, had cautiously laid a
hand on the latch.

The light in the room was dim. Mirepoix had
taken one of the candles with him, and the other
wanted snuffing. I could not see whether the
latch moved; whether or no it was rising. But
watching intently, I made out that the door was
being opened—slowly, noiselessly. I saw some
one enter—a furtive gliding shadow.

8

For a moment I felt nervous; then I recognized the dark hooded figure. It was only Madame d'O. Brave woman! She had evaded the vidame and slipped back to the rescue. Ha, ha! We would defeat the vidame yet! Things were going better.

But then something in her manner — as she stood holding the door and peering into the room — something in her bearing startled and frightened me. As she came forward her movements were so stealthy that her footsteps made no sound. Her dark shadow, moving ahead of her across the floor, was not more silent than she. An undefined desire to make a noise, to give the alarm, seized me.

Half-way across the room she stopped to listen, and looked around, startled herself, I think, by the silence. She could not see her sister, whose figure was blurred by the outlines of the curtain; and no doubt she was puzzled to think what had become of her. The suspense which I felt, but did not understand, was so great that at last I moved, and the bed creaked.

In a moment her face was turned our way, and she glided forward, her features still hidden by the hood of her cloak. She was close to us now, bending over us. She raised her hand to her head, to shade her eyes as she looked more closely, I supposed; and I was wondering whether she saw us — whether she took the shapelessness in the shadow of the curtain for her sister, or could not make it out. I was thinking how we could best apprise her of our presence without alarming her, when Croisette dashed my thoughts to the winds. Croisette, with a tremendous whoop and a crash, bounded over me on to the floor!

She uttered a gasping cry — a cry of intense, awful fear. I have the sound in my ears even now. With that she staggered back, clutching the air. I heard the metallic clang and ring of something falling on the floor. I heard an answering cry of an alarm from the window; and then Madame de Pavannes ran forward and caught her in her arms.

It was strange to find the room lately so silent become at once alive with whispering forms, as we came hastily to light. I cursed Croisette for his folly, and was immeasurably angry with him; but I had no time to waste words on him then. I hurried to the door to guard it. I opened it a hand's breadth and listened. All was quiet below; the house still. I took the key out of the lock and put it in my pocket and went back. Marie and Croisette were standing a little apart from Madame de Pavannes, who, hanging over her sister, was by turns bathing her face and explaining our presence.

In a very few minutes Madame d'O seemed to

recover, and sat up. The first shock of deadly
terror had passed, but she was still pale. She
still trembled, and shrank from meeting our eyes,
though I saw her, when our attention was apparently directed elsewhere, glance at one another
of us with a strange intentness, a shuddering
curiosity. No wonder, I thought. She must
have had a terrible fright—one that might have
killed a more timid woman.

"What on earth did you do that for?" I asked
Croisette, presently, my anger certainly not
decreasing the more I looked at her beautiful
face. "You might have killed her!"

In charity I supposed his nerves had failed
him, for he could not even now give me a
straightforward answer. His only reply was,
"Let us get away! Let us get away from this
horrible house!" and this he kept repeating with
a shudder, as he moved restlessly to and fro.

"With all my heart!" I answered, looking at
him with some contempt. "That is exactly what
we are going to do!"

But all the same his words reminded me of
something which in the excitement of the scene I
had momentarily forgotten, and that was our
duty. Pavannes must still be saved, though not
for Kit; rather to answer to us for his sins. But
he must be saved. And now that the road was
open, every minute lost was a reproach to us.

"Yes," I added, roughly, my thoughts turned into a more rugged channel, "you are right. This is no time for nursing. We must be going. Madame de Pavannes," I went on, addressing myself to her, "you know the way home from here — to your house?"

"Oh, yes," she cried.

"That is well," I answered. "Then we will start. Your sister is sufficiently recovered now, I think. And we will not risk any further delay."

I did not tell her of her husband's danger, or that we suspected him of wronging her, and being in fact the cause of her detention. I wanted her services as a guide. That was the main point, though I was glad to be able to put her in a place of safety at the same time that we fulfilled our own mission.

She rose eagerly. "You are sure that we can get out?" she said.

"Sure," I replied, with a brevity worthy of Bezers himself.

And I was right. We trooped downstairs, making as little noise as possible, with the result that Mirepoix only took the alarm, and came upon us when we were at the outer door, bungling with the lock. Then I made short work of him, checking his scared words of remonstrance by flashing my dagger before his eyes. I induced

him in the same fashion — he was fairly taken by
surprise — to undo the fastenings himself; and
so, bidding him follow us at his peril, we slipped
out one by one. We softly closed the door
behind us. And lo! we were at last free — free
and in the streets of Paris, with the cool night
air fanning our brows. A church hard by tolled
the hour of two, and the strokes were echoed,
before we had gone many steps along the ill-
paved way, by the solemn tones of the bell of
Notre Dame.

We were free and in the streets, with a guide
who knew the way. If Bezers had not gone straight
from us to his vengeance, we might thwart him yet.
I strode along quickly, Madame d'O by my side,
the others a little way in front. Here and there
an oil-lamp, swinging from a pulley in the middle
of the road, enabled us to avoid some obstacle
more foul than usual, or to leap over a pool which
had formed in the kennel. Even in my excitement,
my country-bred senses rebelled against the sights
and smells, the noisome air and oppressive close-
ness of the streets.

The town was quiet, and very dark where the
smoky lamps were not hanging. Yet I wondered
if it ever slept, for more than once we had to stand
aside to give passage to a party of men hurrying
along with links and arms. Several times, too,
especially toward the end of our walk, I was sur-

prised by the flashing of bright lights in a courtyard, the door of which stood half-open to right
or left.   Once I saw the glow of torches reflected
ruddily in the windows of a tall and splendid
mansion, a little withdrawn from the street.   The
source of the light was in the fore-court, hidden
from us by a low wall, but I caught the murmur
of voices and stir of many feet.   Once a gate was
stealthily opened and two armed men looked out,
the act and their manner of doing it reminding
me on the instant of those who had peeped out to
inspect us some hours before in Bezers' house.
And once, nay twice, in the mouth of a narrow
alley, I discerned a knot of men standing motionless in the gloom.   There was an air of mystery
abroad, a feeling as of solemn stir and preparation going on under cover of the darkness, which
awed and unnerved me.

But I said nothing of this, and Madame d'O
was equally silent.   Like most countrymen I was
ready to believe in any exaggeration of the city's
late hours, the more as she made no remark.   I
supposed, shaking off the momentary impression,
that what I saw was innocent and normal.
Besides, I was thinking what I should say to
Pavannes when I saw him, in what terms I should
warn him of his peril, and cast his perfidy in
his teeth.

We had hurried along in this way, and in absolute silence, save when some obstacle or pitfall drew from us an exclamation, for about a quarter of a mile, when my companion, turning into a slightly wider street, slackened her speed, and indicated by a gesture that we had arrived. A lamp hung over the porch, to which she pointed, and showed the small side gate half-open. We were close behind the other three now. I saw Croisette stoop to enter, and as quickly fall back a pace. Why?

In a moment it flashed across my mind that we were too late — that the vidame had been before us.

And yet how quiet it all was!

Then I breathed freely again. I saw that Croisette had only stepped back to avoid some one who was coming out — the coadjutor in fact. The moment the entrance was clear the lad shot in, and the others after him, the priest taking no notice of them, nor they of him.

I was for going in, too, when I felt Madame d'O's hand tighten suddenly on my arm, and then fall from it. Apprised of something by this, I glanced at the priest's face, catching sight of it by chance, just as his eyes met hers. His face was white — nay, it was ugly with disappointment and rage — bitter, snarling rage, that was hardly human. He grasped her by the arm roughly and twisted her round without ceremony, so as to draw her a few paces aside, yet not so far that I could not hear what they said.

"He is not here!" he hissed. "Do you understand? He crossed the river to the Faubourg St. Germain at nightfall — searching for her. And he has not come back! He is on the other side of the water, and midnight has struck this hour past!"

She stood silent for a moment, as if she had received a blow — silent and dismayed. Something serious had happened. I could see that.

"He can not recross the river now?" she said, after a time. "The gates —"

"Shut!" he replied, briefly. "The keys are at the Louvre."

"And the boats are on this side?"

"Every boat!" he answered, striking his one hand on the other with violence. "Every boat! No one may cross until it is over."

"And the Faubourg St. Germain?" she said, in a lower voice.

"There will be nothing done there. Nothing."

CHAPTER VII.

A YOUNG KNIGHT-ERRANT.

I WOULD gladly have left the two together and gone straight into the house. I was eager now to discharge the errand on which I had come so far; and apart from this I had no liking for the priest or wish to overhear his talk. His anger, however, was so patent, and the rudeness with which he treated Madame d'O so pronounced, that I felt I could not leave her with him unless she should dismiss me. So I stood patiently enough — and awkwardly enough too, I dare say — by the door while they talked on in subdued tones. Nevertheless, I felt heartily glad when at length, the discussion ending, madame came back to me. I offered her my arm to help her over the wooden foot of the side gate. She laid her hand on it, but she stood still.

"M. de Caylus," she said, and at that stopped. Naturally I looked at her, and our eyes met. Hers brown and beautiful, shining in the light of the lamp overhead, looked into mine. Her lips were half-parted, and one fair tress of hair had escaped from her hood. "M. de Caylus, will you do me a favor," she resumed, softly, "a favor for which I shall always be grateful?"

I sighed. "Madame," I said, earnestly, for I felt the solemnity of the occasion, "I swear that in ten minutes, if the task I now have in hand be finished I will devote my life to your service. For the present—"

"Well, for the present? But it is the present I want, Master Discretion."

"I must see M. de Pavannes! I am pledged to it," I ejaculated.

"To see M. de Pavannes?"

"Yes."

I was conscious that she was looking at me with eyes of doubt, almost of suspicion.

"Why? why?" she asked with evident surprise. "You have restored — and nearly frightened me to death in doing it — his wife to her home; what more do you want with him, most valiant knight-errant?"

"I must see him," I said, firmly. I would have told her all and been thankful, but the priest was within hearing, or barely out of it; and I had seen too much pass between him and Bezers to be willing to say anything before him.

"You must see M. de Pavannes?" she repeated, gazing at me.

"I must," I replied with decision.

"Then you shall. That is exactly what I am going to help you to do!" she exclaimed. "He is not here. That is what is the matter. He went out at nightfall seeking news of his wife, and crossed the river, the coadjutor says, to the Faubourg St. Germain. Now it is of the utmost importance that he should return before morning —return here.''

''But is he not here?'' I said, finding all my calculations at fault. ''You are sure of it, madame?''

''Quite sure,'' she answered, rapidly. ''Your brothers will have by this time discovered the fact. Now, M. de Caylus, Pavannes must be brought here before morning, not only for his wife's sake — though she will be wild with anxiety — but also —''

''I know,'' I said, eagerly interrupting her, ''for his own, too. There is a danger threatening him.''

She turned swiftly, as if startled, and I turned, and we looked at the priest. I thought we understood one another. ''There is,'' she answered, softly, ''and I would save him from that danger; but he will only be safe, as I happen to know, here! Here, you understand! He must be brought here before daybreak, M. de Caylus. He must! He must!'' she exclaimed, her beautiful features hardening with the earnestness of her feelings. ''And the coadjutor can not go. I can not go. There is only one man who can save him, and that is yourself. There is, above all, not a moment to be lost.''

My thoughts were in a whirl. Even as she spoke she began to walk back the way we had come, her hand on my arm; and I, doubtful, and in a confused way unwilling, went with her. I did not clearly understand the position. I would have wished to go in and confer with Marie and Croisette, but the juncture had occurred so quickly, and it might be that time was as valuable as she said, and — well, it was hard for me, a lad, to refuse her anything when she looked at me with appeal in her eyes. I did manage to stammer, "But I do not know Paris. I could not find my way, I am afraid; and it is night, madame."

She released my arm and stopped. "Night!" she cried, with a scornful ring in her voice. "Night! I thought you were a man, not a boy! You are afraid!"

"Afraid," I said, hotly; "we Cayluses are never afraid."

"Then I can tell you the way, if that be your only difficulty. We turn here. Now, come in with me a moment," she continued, "and I will give you something you will need — and your directions."

She had stopped at the door of a tall, narrow house, standing between larger ones, in a street which appeared to me to be more airy and important than any I had yet seen. As she spoke, she

rang the bell once, twice, thrice. The silvery
tinkle had scarcely died away the third time
before the door opened silently. I saw no one, but
she drew me into a narrow hall or passage. A
taper in an embossed holder was burning on a
chest. She took it up, and telling me to follow
her led the way lightly up the stairs and into a
room, half-parlor, half-bedroom—such a room as
I had never seen before. It was richly hung from
ceiling to floor with blue silk, and lighted by the
soft rays of lamps shaded by Venetian globes of
delicate hues. The scent of cedar wood was in
the air, and on the hearth, in a velvet tray, were
some tiny puppies. A dainty disorder reigned
everywhere. On one table a jewel-case stood
open, on another lay some lace garments, two or
three masks, and a fan. A gemmed riding-whip
and a silver-hilted poniard hung on the same peg.
And, strangest of all, huddled away behind the
door, I espied a plain, black-sheathed sword, and
a man's gauntlets.

She did not wait a moment, but went at once to
the jewel-case. She took from it a gold ring—a
heavy seal ring. She held this out to me in the
most matter-of-fact way, scarcely turning, in
fact. "Put it on your finger," she said, hurriedly.
"If you are stopped by soldiers, or if they will
not give you a boat to cross the river, say boldly
that you are on the king's service. Call for the

officer and show that ring. Play the man. Bid
him stop you at his peril!"

I hastily muttered my thanks, and she as
hastily took something from a drawer and tore it
into strips. Before I knew what she was doing
she was on her knees by me, fastening a white band
of linen round my left sleeve. Then she took my
cap, and with the same precipitation fixed a fragment of the stuff in it, in the form of a rough
cross.

"There," she said. "Now, listen, M. de Caylus. There is more afoot to-night than you know
of. Those badges will help you across to St.
Germain, but the moment you land tear them off.
Tear them off, remember. They will help you no
longer. You will come back by the same boat,
and will not need them. If you are seen to wear
them as you return, they will command no respect,
but, on the contrary, will bring you — and perhaps me — into trouble."

"I understand," I said, "but—"

"You must ask no questions," she retorted,
waving one snowy finger before my eyes. "My
knight-errant must have faith in me, as I have in
him, or he would not be here at this time of night,
and alone with me. But remember this also.
When you meet Pavannes do not say you come
from me. Keep that in your mind; I will explain
the reason afterward. Say merely that his wife

is found, and is wild with anxiety about him. If
you say anything as to his danger he may refuse
to come. Men are obstinate.''

I nodded a smiling assent, thinking I understood. At the same time I permitted myself in
my own mind a little discretion. Pavannes was
not a fool, and the name of the vidame—but,
however, I should see. I had more to say to him
than she knew of. Meanwhile she explained very
carefully the three turnings I had to take to reach
the river, and the wharf where boats most commonly lay, and the name of the house in which I
should find M. de Pavannes.

"He is at the Hotel de Bailli,'' she said. '' And
there, I think that is all.''

"No, not all,'' I said, hardily. "There is one
thing I have not got. And that is a sword!''

She followed the direction of my eyes, started,
and laughed—a little oddly. But she fetched
the weapon. "Take it, and do not,'' she urged,
"do not lose time. Do not mention me to Pavannes. Do not let the white badges be seen as
you return. *That* is really all. And now good
luck!'' She gave me her hand to kiss. "Good
luck, my knight-errant, good luck—and come
back to me soon!''

She smiled divinely, it seemed to me, as she
said these last words, and the same smile followed
me downstairs; for she leaned over the stair-head

with one of the lamps in her hand and directed
me how to draw the bolts.   I took one backward
glance as I did so at the fair stooping figure above
me, the shining eyes and tiny outstretched hand,
and then darting into the gloom I hurried on my
way.

I was in a strange mood. A few minutes before
I had been at Pavannes' door, at the end of our
journey; on the verge of success.   I had been
within an ace, as I supposed at least, of executing
my errand.   I had held the cup of success in my
hand.   And it had slipped.   Now the conflict had
to be fought over again; the danger to be faced.
It would have been no more than natural if I had
felt the disappointment keenly; if I had almost
despaired.

But it was otherwise — far otherwise.   Never
had my heart beat higher or more proudly than as
I now hurried through the streets, avoiding such
groups as were abroad in them, and intent only
on observing the proper turnings.   Never in any
moment of triumph in after days, in love or war,
did anything like the exhilaration, the energy, the
spirit, of those minutes come back to me.   I had
a woman's badge in my cap — for the first time —
the music of her voice in my ears.   I had a magic
ring on my finger, a talisman on my arm.   My
sword was at my side again.   All round me lay a
misty city of adventures, of danger and romance,

9

full of the richest and most beautiful possibilities;
a city of real witchery, such as I had read of in
stories, through which those fairy gifts and my
right hand should guide me safely.   I did not even
regret my brothers, or our separation.   I was the
eldest.   It was fitting that the cream of the enterprise should be reserved for me, Anne de Caylus.
And to what might it not lead?   In fancy I saw
myself already a duke and peer of France; already
I held the baton.

Yet while I exulted boyishly, I did not forget
what I was about.   I kept my eyes open, and soon
remarked that the number of people passing to and
fro in the dark streets had much increased within
the last half-hour.   The silence in which in groups
or singly these figures stole by me was very striking.   I heard no brawling, fighting or singing; yet
if it were too late for these things, why were so
many people up and about?   I began to count
presently, and found that at least half of those I
met wore badges in their hats and on their arms,
similar to mine, and that they all moved with a
business-like air, as if bound for some rendezvous.

I was not a fool, though I was young, and in
some matters less quick than Croisette.   The hints
which had been dropped by so many had not been
lost on me.   "There is more afoot to-night than
you know of," Madame d'O had said.   And having eyes as well as ears, I fully believed it.   Some-

thing was afoot. Something was going to happen
in Paris before morning. But what, I wondered.
Could it be that a rebellion was about to break
out? If so I was on the king's service, and all was
well. I might even be going—and only eighteen
—to make history! Or was it only a brawl on a
great scale between two parties of nobles? I had
heard of such things happening in Paris. Then
—well, I did not see how I could act in that case.
I must be guided by events.

I did not imagine anything else which it could
be. That is the truth, though it may need explanation. I was accustomed only to the milder
religious differences, the more evenly balanced
parties of Quercy, where the peace between the
Catholics and Huguenots had been welcome to all
save a very few. I could not gauge, therefore, the
fanaticism of the Parisian populace, and lost
count of the factor which made possible that
which was going to happen—was going to happen
in Paris before daylight as surely as the sun was
going to rise! I knew that the Huguenot nobles
were present in the city in great numbers, but it
did not occur to me that they could as a body be
in danger. They were many and powerful, and
as was said, in favor with the king. They were
under the protection of the King of Navarre—
France's brother-in-law of a week, and the Prince
of Condé; and though these princes were young,

Coligny, the sagacious admiral, was old, and not much the worse, I had learned, for his wound. He at least was high in royal favor, a trusted counselor. Had not the king visited him on his sickbed and sat by him for an hour together?

Surely, I thought, if there were danger, these men would know of it. And then the Huguenots' main enemy, Henri le Balafré, the splendid Duke of Guise, "our great man," and "Lorraine," as the crowd called him — he, it was rumored, was in disgrace at court. In a word, these things, to say nothing of the peaceful and joyous occasion which had brought the Huguenots to Paris, and which seemed to put treachery out of the question, were more than enough to prevent me forecasting the event.

If for a moment, indeed, as I hurried along toward the river, anything like the truth occurred to me, I put it from me. I say with pride, I put it from me as a thing impossible. For, God forbid — one may speak out the truth these forty years back — God forbid, say I, that all Frenchmen should bear the blood-guiltiness which came of other than French brains, though French were the hands that did the work.

I was not greatly troubled by my forebodings therefore; and the state of exaltation to which Madame d'O's confidence had raised my spirits lasted until one of the narrow streets by the

Louvre brought me suddenly within sight of the
river. Here faint moonlight, bursting momentarily through the clouds, was shining on the placid
surface of the water. The fresh air played upon,
and cooled my temples. And this was the quiet
scene so abruptly presented to me, gave check to
my thoughts, and somewhat sobered me.

At some distance to my left I could distinguish
in the middle of the river the pile of buildings
which crowd the Ile de la Cité, and could follow
the nearer arm of the stream as it swept land-
ward of these, closely hemmed in by houses, but
unbroken as yet by the arches of the Pont Neuf,
which I have lived to see built. Not far from me,
on my right — indeed, within a stone's throw —
the bulky mass of the Louvre rose dark and
shapeless against the sky. Only a narrow open
space — the foreshore — separated me from the
water, beyond which I could see an irregular line
of buildings, that no doubt formed the Faubourg
St. Germain.

I had been told that I should find stairs leading
down to the water, and boats moored at the foot
of them, at this point. Accordingly I walked
quickly across the open space to a spot, where I
made out a couple of posts set up on the brink —
doubtless to mark the landing place.

I had not gone ten paces, however, out of the
shadow, before I chanced to look around, and

discerned, with an unpleasant feeling, three
figures detach themselves from it and advance in
a row behind me, so as the better to cut off my
retreat.   I was not to succeed in my enterprise
too easily, then.   That was clear.   Still I thought
it better to act as if I had not seen my followers,
and, collecting myself, I walked as quickly as I
could down to the steps.   The three were by that
time close upon me — within striking distance
almost.   I turned abruptly and confronted them.

"Who are you, and what do want?" I said,
eyeing them warily, my hand on my sword.

They did not answer, but separated more widely
so as to form a half-circle, and one of them
whistled.   On the instant a knot of men started
out of the line of houses, and came quickly across
the strip of light toward us.

The position seemed serious.   If I could have
run indeed — but I glanced round, and found
escape in that fashion impossible.   There were
men crouching on the steps behind me, between
me and the river.   I had fallen into a trap.
Indeed, there was nothing for it now but to do as
madame had bidden me, and play the man boldly.
I had the words still ringing in my ears.   I had
enough of the excitement I had lately felt still
bounding in my veins to give nerve and daring.
I folded my arms and drew myself up.

"Knaves!" I said, with as much quiet contempt

as I could muster, "you mistake me. You do not know whom you have to deal with. Get me a boat, and let two of you row me across. Hinder me, and your necks shall answer for it — or your backs!"

A laugh and an oath of derision formed the only response, and before I could add more, the larger group arrived and joined the three.

"Who is it, Pierre?" asked one of these in a matter-of-fact way, which showed I had not fallen among mere thieves.

The speaker seemed to be the leader of the band. He had a feather in his bonnet, and I saw a steel corselet gleam under his cloak when some one held up a lantern to examine me the better. His trunk-hose were striped with black, white, and green — the livery, as I learned afterward, of Monsieur the King's brother, the Duke of Anjou, afterward Henry the Third; then a close friend of the Duke of Guise, and later his murderer. The captain spoke with a foreign accent, and his complexion was dark to swarthiness. His eyes sparkled and flashed like black beads. It was easy to see that he was an Italian.

"A gallant young cock enough," the soldier who had whistled answered, "and not quite of the breed we expected." He held his lantern toward me and pointed to the white badge on my sleeve. "It strikes me we have caught a crow instead of a pigeon!"

"How comes this?" the Italian asked, harshly, addressing me. "Who are you? And why do you wish to cross the river at this time of night, young sir?"

I acted on the inspiration of the moment. "Play the man boldly!" madame had said. I would, and I did with a vengeance. I sprang forward and, seizing the captain by the clasp of his cloak, shook him violently, and flung him off with all my force, so that he reeled. "Dog!" I exclaimed, advancing as if I would seize him again. "Learn how to speak to your betters! Am I to be stopped by such sweepings as you? Hark ye, I am on the king's service!"

He fairly spluttered with rage. "More like the devil's!" he exclaimed, pronouncing his words abominably, and fumbling vainly for his weapon. "King's service or no service, you do not insult Andrea Pallavicini!"

I could only vindicate my daring by greater daring, and I saw this even as, death staring me in the face, my heart seemed to stop. The man had his mouth open and his hand raised to give an order which would certainly have sent Anne de Caylus from the world, when I cried passionately — it was my last chance, and I never wished to live more strongly than at that moment — I cried passionately, "Andrea Pallavicini, if such be your name, look at that! Look at that!" I repeated, shaking my open hand with the ring on it before his face, "and then hinder me if you dare! To-morrow if you have quarterings enough, I will see to your quarrel! Now send me on my way, or your fate be on your own head! Disobey — ay, do but hesitate — and I will call on these very men of yours to cut you down!"

It was a bold throw, for I staked all on a talisman of which I did not know the value! To me it was the turn of a die, for I had had no leisure to look at the ring, and knew no more than a babe whose it was. But the venture was as happy as desperate.

Andrea Pallavicini's expression — no pleasant one at the best of times — changed on the instant. His face fell as he seized my hand, and peered at the ring long and intently. Then he cast a quick glance of suspicion at his men, of hatred at me. But I cared nothing for his glance, or his hatred. I saw already that he had made up his mind to obey the charm, and that for me was everything. "If you had shown that to me a little earlier, young sir, it would, may be, have been better for both of us," he said, a surly menace in his voice. And cursing his men for their stupidity, he ordered two of them to unmoor a boat.

Apparently the craft had been secured with more care than skill, for to loosen it seemed to be a work of time. Meanwhile I stood waiting in the midst of the group, anxious and yet exultant; an object of curiosity, and yet curious myself. I heard the guards whisper together, and caught such phrases as, "It is the Duc d'Aumale."

"No, it is not D'Aumale. It is nothing like him."

"Well, he has the duke's ring, fool!"

"The duke's?"

"Ay."

"Then it is all right, God bless him!" This last was uttered with extreme fervor.

I was conscious too of being the object of many respectful glances; and had just bidden the men on the steps below me to be quick, when I discovered with alarm three figures moving across the open space toward us, and coming apparently from the same point from which Pallavicini and his men had emerged.

In a moment I foresaw danger. "Now be quick there!" I cried again. But scarcely had I spoken before I saw that it was impossible to get afloat before these others came up, and I prepared to stand my ground resolutely.

The first words, however, with which Pallavicini saluted the newcomers scattered my fears. "Well, what the foul fiend do you want?" he exclaimed, rudely; and he rapped out half a dozen *corpos* before they could answer him. "What have you brought him here for, when I left him in the guardhouse? Imbeciles!"

"Captain Pallavicini," interposed the midmost of the three, speaking with patience — he was a man of about thirty, dressed with some richness, though his clothes were now disordered as though by a struggle — "I have induced these good men to bring me down —"

"Then," cried the captain, brutally interrupting him, "you have lost your labor, monsieur."

"You do not know me," replied the prisoner with sternness — a prisoner he seemed to be. "You do not understand that I am a friend of the Prince of Conde, and that —"

He would have said more, but the Italian again cut him short. "A fig for the Prince of Condé!" he cried; "I understand my duty. You may as well take things easily. You can not cross, and you can not go home, and you can not have any explanation; except that it is the king's will! Explanation," he grumbled, in a lower tone, "you will get it soon enough, I warrant! Before you want it!"

"But there is a boat going to cross," said the other, controlling his temper by an effort and speaking with dignity. "You told me that by the king's order no one could cross; and you arrested me because, having urgent need to visit St. Germain, I persisted. Now what does this mean, Captain Pallavincini? Others are crossing. I ask what this means?"

"Whatever you please, M. de Pavannes," the Italian retorted contemptuously. "Explain it for yourself!"

I started as the name struck my ear, and at once cried out in surprise, "M. de Pavannes!" Had I heard aright?

Apparently I had, for the prisoner turned to me with a bow. "Yes, sir," he said, with dignity, "I am M. de Pavannes. I have not the honor of knowing you, but you seem to be a gentleman." He cast a withering glance at the captain as he said this. "Perhaps you will explain to me why this violence has been done to me. If you can, I shall consider it a favor; if not, pardon me."

I did not answer him at once, for a good reason — that every faculty I had was bent on a close scrutiny of the man himself. He was fair, and of a ruddy complexion. His beard was cut in the sharp pointed fashion of the court; and in these respects he bore a kind of likeness, a curious likeness, to Louis de Pavannes. But his figure was shorter and stouter. He was less martial in bearing, with more of the air of a scholar than a soldier. "You are related to M. Louis de Pavannes?" I said, my heart beginning to beat with an odd excitement. I think I foresaw already what was coming.

"I am Louis de Pavannes," he replied, with impatience.

I stared at him in silence, thinking — thinking — thinking. And then I said, slowly, "You have a cousin of the same name?"

"I have."

"He fell prisoner to the Vicomte de Caylus at Moncontour?"

"He did," he answered, curtly. "But what of that, sir?"

Again I did not answer — at once. The murder was out. I remembered, in the dim fashion in which one remembers such things after the event, that I had heard Louis de Pavannes, when we first became acquainted with him, mention this cousin of the same name; the head of a younger branch. But our Louis living in Provence and the other in Normandy, the distance between their homes and the troubles of the times had loosened a tie which their common religion might have strengthened. They had scarcely ever seen one another. As Louis had spoken of his name-sake but once during his long stay with us, and I had not foreseen the connection to be formed between our families, it was no wonder that in the coarse of months the chance word had passed out of my head, and I had clean forgotten the subject of it.

Here, however, he was before my eyes, and seeing him, I saw too what the discovery meant. It meant a most joyful thing — a most wonderful

thing which I longed to tell Croisette and Marie.
It meant that our Louis de Pavannes — my cheek
burned for my want of faith in him — was no
villain after all, but such a noble gentleman as we
had always till this day thought him. It meant
that he was no court gallant bent on breaking a
country heart for sport, but Kit's own true lover!
And — and it meant more — it meant that he was
yet in danger, and still ignorant of the vow that
unchained fiend Bezers had taken to have his life!
In pursuing his namesake we had been led astray,
how sadly I only knew now. And had indeed
lost most precious time.

"Your wife, M. de Pavannes —" I began in
haste, seeing the necessity of explaining matters
with the utmost quickness. "Your wife is —"

"Ah, my wife!" he cried, interrupting me, with
anxiety in his tone. "What of her? You have
seen her?"

"I have. She is safe at your house in the Rue
de St. Merri."

"Thank heaven for that!" he replied, fervently.
Before he could say more Captain Andrea interrupted us. I could see that his suspicions were
aroused afresh. He pushed rudely between us,
and addressing me said, "Now, young sir, your
boat is ready."

"My boat?" I answered, while I rapidly considered the situation. Of course I did not want

to cross the river now. No doubt Pavannes —
this Pavannes — could guide me to Louis' address.
"My boat?"

"Yes, it is waiting," the Italian replied, his
black eyes roving from one to the other of us.

"Then let it wait," I answered, haughtily,
speaking with an assumption of anger. "Plague
upon you for interrupting us! I shall not cross the
river now. This gentleman can give me the infor-
mation I want. I shall take him back with me."

"To whom?"

"To whom? To those who sent me, sirrah!"
I thundered. "You do not seem to be much in
the duke's confidence, Captain," I went on.
"Now take a word of advice from me! There is
nothing so easily cast off as an over-officious servant! He goes too far — and he goes like an old
glove. An old glove," I repeated, grimly, sneer-
ing in his face, "which saves the hand and
suffers itself. Beware of too much zeal, Captain
Pallavicini! It is a dangerous thing!"

He turned pale with anger at being thus
treated by a beardless boy. But he faltered all
the same. What I said was unpleasant, but the
bravo knew it was true.

I saw the impression I had made, and I turned
to the soldiers standing round.

"Bring here, my friends," I said, "M. de
Pavannes' sword."

One ran up to the guard-house and brought it
at once. They were towns-folk, burgher guards,
or such like, and for some reason betrayed so
evident a respect for me, that I soberly believe
they would have turned on their temporary leader
at my bidding. Pavannes took his sword and
placed it under his arm. We both bowed cere-
moniously to Pallavicini, who scowled in response,
and slowly, for I was afraid to show any signs of
haste, we walked across the moonlit space to the
bottom of the street by which I had come. There
the gloom swallowed us up at once. Pavannes
touched my sleeve and stopped in the darkness.

"I beg to be allowed to thank you for your
aid," he said, with emotion, turning and facing
me. "Whom have I the honor of addressing?"

"M. Anne de Caylus, a friend of your cousin,"
I replied.

"Indeed?" he said. "Well, I thank you most
heartily;" and we embraced with warmth.

"But I could have done little," I answered
modestly, "on your behalf, if it had not been for
this ring."

"And the virtue of the ring lies in —?"

"In — I am sure I can not say in what," I con-
fessed. And then, in the sympathy which the
scene had naturally created between us, I forgot
one portion of my lady's commands and I added
impulsively, "All I know is that Madame d'O

gave it me; and that it has done all, and more than all, she said it would."

"Who gave it to you?" he asked, grasping my arm so tightly as to hurt me.

"Madame d'O," I repeated. It was too late to draw back now.

"That woman!" he ejaculated in a strange, low whisper. "Is it possible? That woman gave it you?"

I wondered what on earth he meant, surprise, scorn, and dislike were so blended in his tone. It even seemed to me that he drew off from me somewhat. "Yes, M. de Pavannes," I replied, offended and indignant; "it is so far possible that it is the truth; and more, I think you would not so speak of this lady if you knew all, and that it was through her your wife was to-day freed from those who were detaining her, and taken safely home!"

"Ha!" he cried, eagerly. "Then where has my wife been?"

"At the house of Mirepoix, the glover," I answered, coldly, "in the Rue Platriére. Do you know him? You do? Well, she was kept there a prisoner until we helped her to escape an hour or so ago."

He did not seem to comprehend even then. I could see little of his face, but there was doubt and wonder in his tone when he spoke. "Mire-

10

poix, the glover," he murmured. "He is an
honest man enough, though a Catholic. She was
kept there! Who kept her there?"

"The Abbess of the Ursulines seems to have
been at the bottom of it," I explained, fretting
with impatience. This wonder was misplaced, I
thought, and time was passing. "Madame d'O
found out where she was," I continued, "and took
her home, and then sent me to fetch you, hearing
you had crossed the river. That is the story in
brief."

"That woman sent you to fetch me?" he repeated again.

"Yes," I answered, angrily. "She did, M. de
Pavannes."

"Then," he said, slowly, and with an air of
solemn conviction which could not but impress
me, "there is a trap laid for me! She is the worst,
the most wicked, the vilest of women! If she
sent you, this is a trap! And my wife has fallen
into it already! Heaven help her—and me—if
it be so!"

CHAPTER VIII.

THE PARISIAN MATINS.

THERE are some statements for which it is impossible to be prepared; statements so strong and so startling that it is impossible to answer them except by action — by a blow. And this of M. de Pavannes was one of these. If there had been any one present, I think I should have given him the lie and drawn upon him. But alone with him at midnight, in the shadow near the bottom of the Rue des Fosses, with no witnesses, with every reason to feel friendly toward him, what was I to do?

As a fact, I did nothing. I stood, silent and stupefied, waiting to hear more. He did not keep me long.

"She is my wife's sister," he continued, grimly. "But I have no reason to shield her on that account. Shield her? Had you lived at court only a month I might shield her all I could, M. de Caylus, it would avail nothing. Not Madame de Sauves is better known. And I would not if I could! I know well, though my wife will not believe it, that there is nothing so near Madame d'O's heart as to get rid of her sister and me — of both of us — that she may succeed to Madeleine's

(147)

inheritance! Oh, yes, I had good grounds for
being nervous yesterday, when my wife did not
return," he added, excitedly.

"But there at least you wrong Madame d'O!"
I cried, shocked and horrified by an accusation,
which seemed so much more dreadful in the silence
and gloom — and withal so much less preposter-
ous than it might have seemed in the daylight.
"There you certainly wrong her! For shame!
M. de Pavannes."

He came a step nearer, and laying a hand on
my sleeve peered into my face. "Did you see a
priest with her?" he asked, slowly. "A man
called the coadjutor — a down-looking dog?"

I said — with a shiver of dread, a sudden revul-
sion of feeling, born of his manner — that I had.
And I explained the part the priest had taken.

"Then," Pavannes rejoined, "I am right.
There *is* a trap laid for me. The Abbess of the
Ursulines! She abduct my wife? Why she is her
dearest friend, believe me. It is impossible. She
would be more likely to save her from danger
than to — umph! wait a minute." I did; I waited,
dreading what he might discover, until he muttered, checking himself — "Can that be it? Can
it be that the abbess did know of some danger
threatening us, and would have put Madeleine in
a safe retreat? I wonder!"

And I wondered; and then — well, thoughts

are like gunpowder; the least spark will fire a train. His words were few, but they formed spark enough to raise such a flare in my brain as for a moment blinded me, and shook me so that I trembled. The shock over, I was left face to face with a possibility of wickedness such as I could never have suspected of myself. I remembered Mirepoix's distress and the priest's eagerness. I recalled the gruff warning Bezers—even Bezers, and there was something very odd in Bezers giving a warning!—had given Madame de Pavannes when he told her that she would be better where she was. I thought of the wakefulness which I had marked in the streets, the silent hurrying to and fro, the signs of coming strife, and contrasted these with the quietude and seeming safety of Mirepoix's house; and I hastily asked Pavannes at what time he had been arrested.

"About an hour before midnight," he answered.

"Then you know nothing of what is happening?" I replied, quickly. "Why, even while we are loitering here—but listen!"

And with all speed, stammering indeed in my haste and anxiety, I told him what I had noticed in the streets, and the hints I had heard, and I showed him the badges with which madame had furnished me.

His manner when he had heard me out frightened me still more. He drew me on in a kind of fury to a house in the windows of which some lighted candles had appeared not a minute before. "The ring!" he cried, "let me see the ring! Whose is it?"

He held up my hand to this chance light and we looked at the ring. It was a heavy gold signet, with one curious characteristic; it had two facets. On one of these was engraved the letter "H," and above it a crown. On the other was an eagle with outstretched wings.

Pavannes let my hand drop and leaned against the wall in sudden despair. "It is the Duke of Guise's," he muttered. "It is the eagle of Lorraine."

"Ha!" said I, softly, seeing light. The duke was the idol then, as later, of the Parisian populace, and I understood now why the citizen soldiers had shown me such respect. They had taken me for the duke's envoy and confidant.

But I saw no farther. Pavannes did, and murmured bitterly, "We may say our prayers, we Huguenots. That is our death-warrant. To-morrow night there will not be one left in Paris, lad. Guise has his father's death to avenge, and these cursed Parisians will do his bidding like the wolves they are! The Baron de Rosny warned us of this, word for word. I would to heaven we had taken his advice!"

"Stay!" I cried — he was going too fast for me — "stay!" His monstrous conception, though it marched some way with my own suspicions, out-ran them far. I saw no sufficient grounds for it. "The king — the king would not permit such a thing, M. de Pavannes," I argued.

"Boy, you are blind!" he rejoined, impatiently, for now he saw all and I nothing. "Yonder was the Duke of Anjou's captain — Monsieur's officer, the follower of France's brother, mark you! And *he* — he obeyed the duke's ring! The duke has a free hand to-night, and he hates us. And the river. Why are we not to cross the river? The king indeed! The king has undone us. He has sold us to his brother and the Guises. *Va chasser l' Idole*" — for the second time I heard the quaint phrase, which I learned afterward was an anagram of the king's name, Charles de Valois, used by the Protestants as a password — "*Va chasser l' Idole* has betrayed us! I remember the very words he used to the admiral, 'Now we have got you here we shall not let you go so easily!' Oh, the traitor! The wretched traitor!"

He leaned against the wall, overcome by the horror of the conviction which had burst upon him, and unnerved by the imminence of the peril. At all times he was an unready man, I fancy, more fit, courage apart, for the college than the field, and now he gave way to despair. Perhaps the thought of his wife unmanned him. **Perhaps** the excitement through which he had already gone tended to stupefy him, or the suddenness of the discovery.

At any rate, I was the first to gather my wits together, and my earliest impulse was to tear into two parts a white handkerchief I had in my pouch, and fasten one to his sleeve, the other in his hat, in rough imitation of the badges I wore myself.

It will appear from this that I no longer trusted Madame d'O. I was not convinced, it is true, of her conscious guilt, still I did not trust her entirely. "Do not wear them on your return," she had said and that was odd; although I could not yet believe that she was such a siren as Father Pierre had warned us of, telling tales from old poets. Yet I doubted, shuddering as I did so. Her companionship with that vile priest, her strange eagerness to secure Pavannes' return, her mysterious directions to me, her anxiety to take her sister home — home, where she would be exposed to danger, as being in a known Huguenot's house — these things pointed to but one conclusion, still that one was so horrible that I would not, even while I doubted and distrusted her, I would not, I could not accept it. I put it from me, and refused to believe it, although during the rest of that night it kept coming back to me and knocking for admission at my brain.

All this flashed through my mind while I was
fixing on Pavannes' badges. Not that I lost time
about it, for from the moment I grasped the position as he conceived it, every minute we had
wasted on explanations seemed to me an hour.
I reproached myself for having forgotten even for
an instant that which had brought us to town —
the rescue of Kit's lover. We had small chance
now of reaching him in time, misled as we had
been by this miserable mistake in identity. If
my companion's fears were well-founded, Louis
would fall in the general massacre of the Huguenots, probably before we could reach him. If
ill-founded, still we had small reason to hope.
Bezers' vengeance would not wait. I knew him
too well to think it. A Guise might spare his
foe, but the vidame — the vidame never! He
had warned Madame de Pavannes it was true;
but that abnormal exercise of benevolence could
only, I cynically thought, have the more exasper-
ated the devil within him, which now would be
ravening like a dog disappointed of its victuals.

I glanced up at the line of sky visible between
the tall houses, and lo! the dawn was coming. It
wanted scarcely half an hour of daylight, though
down in the dark streets about us the night still
reigned. Yes, the morning was coming, bright
and hopeful, and the city was quiet. There were
no signs, no sounds of riot or disorder. Surely,

I thought, surely Pavannes must be mistaken. Either the plot had never existed, that was most likely, or it had been abandoned, or perhaps — crack!

A pistol shot! Short, sharp, ominous it rang out on the instant, a solitary sound in the night! It was somewhere near us, and I stopped. I had been speaking to my companion at the moment. "Where was it?" I cried, looking behind me.

"Close to us. Near the Louvre," he answered, listening intently. "See! See! Ah, heavens!" he continued in a voice of despair, "it was a signal!"

It was. One, two, three! Before I could count so far, lights sprang into brightness in the windows of nine out of ten houses in the short street where we stood, as if lighted by a single hand. Before, too, I could count as many more, or ask him what this meant; before indeed, we could speak or stir from the spot, or think what we should do, with a hurried clang and clash, as if brought into motion by furious, frenzied hands, a great bell just above our heads began to boom and whirr. It hurled its notes into space, it suddenly filled all the silence. It dashed its harsh sounds down upon the trembling city till the air heaved, and the houses about us rocked. It made in an instant a pandemonium of the quiet night.

We turned and hurried instinctively from the place, crouching and amazed, looking upward with bent shoulders and scared faces. "What is it? what is it?" I cried, half in resentment, half in terror. It deafened me.

"The bell of St. Germain l'Auxerrois!" he shouted in answer. "The church of the Louvre. It is as I said. We are doomed!"

"Doomed? No!" I replied fiercely, for my courage seemed to rise again on the wave of sound and excitement as if rebounding from the momentary shock. "Never! We wear the devil's livery, and he will look after his own. Draw, man, and let him that stops us look to himself. You know the way. Lead on!" I cried, savagely.

He caught the infection and drew his sword. So we started boldly, and the result justified my confidence. We looked, no doubt, as like murderers as any who were abroad that night. Moving in this desperate guise we hastened up that street and into another — still pursued by the din and clangor of the bell — and then a short distance along a third. We were not stopped or addressed by any one, though numbers, increasing each moment as door after door opened, and we drew nearer to the heart of the commotion, were hurrying in the same direction, side by side with us; and though in front, where now and again lights gleamed on a mass of weapons, or on

white eager faces, filling some alley from wall to
wall, we heard the roar of voices rising and falling like the murmur of an angry sea.

All was blurr, hurry, confusion, tumult. Yet
I remember, as we pressed onward with the
stream and part of it, certain sharp outlines. I
caught here and there a glimpse of a pale scared
face at a window, a half-clad form at a door, of
the big, wondering eyes of a child held up to see
us pass, of a Christ at a corner ruddy in the
smoky glare of a link, of a woman armed, and
in man's clothes, who walked some distance side
by side with us, and led off a ribald song. I
retain a memory of these things; of brief bursts
of light and long intervals of darkness, and
always, as we tramped forward, my hand on
Pavannes' sleeve, of an ever-growing tumult in
front—an ever-rising flood of noise.

At last we came to a standstill where a side
street ran out of ours. Into this the hurrying
throng tried to wheel, and, unable to do so,
halted, and pressed about the head of the street,
which was already full to overflowing; and so
fought with hungry eyes for places whence they
might look down it. Pavannes and I struggled
only to get through the crowd—to get on; but
the efforts of those behind partly aiding and
partly thwarting our own, presently forced us to
a position whence we could not avoid seeing what
was afoot.

The street—this side street—was ablaze with light. From end to end every gable, every hatchment was glowing, every window was flickering in the glare of torches. It was paved too with faces—human faces, yet scarcely human—all looking one way, all looking upward; and the noise, as from time to time this immense crowd groaned or howled in unison, like a wild beast in its fury, was so appalling, that I clutched Pavannes' arm and clung to him in momentary terror. I do not wonder now that I quailed, though sometimes I have heard that sound since. For there is nothing in the world so dreadful as that brute beast we call the *canaille*, when the chain is off and its cowardly soul is roused.

Near our end of the street a group of horsemen, rising island-like from the sea of heads, sat motionless in their saddles about a gateway. They were silent, taking no notice of the rioting fiends shouting at their girths, but watching in grim quiet what was passing within the gates. They were handsomely dressed, although some wore corselets over their satin coats or lace above buff jerkins. I could even at that distance see the jewels gleam in the bonnet of one who seemed to be their leader. He was in the center of the band, a very young man, perhaps twenty or twenty-one, of most splendid presence, sitting his horse superbly. He wore a gray riding-coat, and was a head taller than any of his companions. There was pride in the very air with which his horse bore him.

I did not need to ask Pavannes who he was. I *knew* that he was the Duke of Guise, and that the house before which he stood was Coligny's. I knew what was being done there. And in the same moment I sickened with horror and rage. I had a vision of gray hairs and blood and fury scarcely human. And I rebelled. I battled with the rabble about me. I forced my way through them tooth and nail after Pavannes, intent only on escaping, only on getting away from there. And so we neither halted nor looked back until we were clear of the crowd, and had left the blaze of light and the work doing by it some way behind us.

We found ourselves then in the mouth of an obscure alley which my companion whispered would bring us to his house, and here we paused to take breath and look back. The sky was red behind us, the air full of the clash and din of the tocsin, and the flood of sounds which poured from every tower and steeple. From the eastward came the rattle of drums and random shots, and shrieks of "*A bas Coligny!*" "*A bas les Huguenots!*" Meanwhile the city was rising as one man, pale at this dread awakening. From every window men and women, frightened by the uproar, were craning their necks, asking or answering questions or hurriedly calling for and kindling tapers. But as yet the general populace seemed to be taking no active part in the disorder.

Pavannes raised his hat an instant as we stood in the shadow of the houses. "The noblest man in France is dead," he said, softly and reverently. "God rest his soul! They have had their way with him, and killed him like a dog! He was an old man, and they did not spare him! A noble, and they have called in the *canaille* to tear him! But be sure, my friend," and as the speaker's tone changed, and grew full and proud, his form seemed to swell with it; "be sure the cruel shall not live out half their days! No. He that takes the knife shall perish by the knife! And go to his own place! I shall not see it, but you will!"

His words made no great impression on me then. My hardihood was returning. I was throbbing with fierce excitement, and tingling for the fight. But years afterward, when the two who stood highest in the group about Coligny's threshold died, the one at thirty-eight, the other at thirty-five — when Henry of Guise and Henry of Valois died within six months of one another by the assassin's knife — I remembered Pavannes' augury. And remembering it, I read the ways of Providence, and saw that the very audacity of which Guise took advantage to entrap Coligny led

him too in his turn to trip, smiling and bowing, a
comfit box in his hand, and the kisses of his mistress damp on his lips, into a king's closet, a
king's closet at Blois! Led him to lift the curtain
—ah! to lift the curtain, what Frenchman does not
know the tale? — behind which stood the admiral!

To return to our own fortunes: After a hurried
glance we resumed our way, and sped through the
alley, holding a brief consultation as we went.
Pavannes' first hasty instinct to seek shelter at
home began to lose its force, and he to consider
whether his return would not endanger his wife.
The mob might be expected to spare her, he
argued. Her death would not benefit any private
foes if he escaped. He was for keeping away
therefore. But I would not agree to this. The
priest's crew of desperadoes, assuming Pavannes'
suspicions to be correct, would wait some time,
no doubt, to give the master of the house a
chance to return, but would certainly attack
sooner or later out of greed, if from no other
motive. Then the lady's fate would at the best
be uncertain. I was anxious myself to rejoin my
brothers, and take all future chances, whether of
saving our Louis, or escaping ourselves, with
them. United we should be four good swords,
and might at least protect Madame de Pavannes
to a place of safety, if no opportunity of succor-
ing Louis should present itself. We had too, the

duke's ring, and this might be of service at a
pinch.   "No," I urged, "let us get together.
We two will slip in at the front gate, and bolt
and bar it, and then we will all escape in a body
at the back, while they are forcing the gateway."

"There is no door at the back," he answered,
shaking his head.

"There are windows?"

"They are too strongly barred.   We could
not break out in the time," he explained, with a
groan.

I paused at that, crestfallen.   But danger
quickened my wits.   In a moment I had another
plan, not so hopeful and more dangerous, yet
worth trying I thought.   I told him of it, and he
agreed to it.   As he nodded assent we emerged
into a street, and I saw, for the gray light of
morning was beginning to penetrate between the
houses, that we were only a few yards from the
gateway, and the small door by which I had seen
my brothers enter.   Were they still in the house?
Were they safe?   I had been away an hour at
least.

Anxious as I was about them, I looked around
me very keenly as we flitted across the road, and
knocked gently at the door.   I thought it so
likely that we should be fallen upon here, that I
stood on my guard while we waited.   But we
were not molested.   The street, being at some

11

distance from the center of the commotion, was still and empty, with no signs of life apparent except the rows of heads poked through the windows — all possessing eyes which watched us heedfully and in perfect silence. Yes, the street was quite empty, except — except, ah! except, for that lurking figure, which, even as I espied it, shot round a distant angle of the wall, and was lost to sight.

"There!" I cried, reckless now who might hear me, "knock! knock louder! never mind the noise. The alarm is given. A score of people are watching us, and yonder spy has gone off to summon his friends."

The truth was my anger was rising. I could bear no longer the silent regards of all those eyes at the windows. I writhed under them — cruel, pitiless eyes they were. I read in them a morbid curiosity, a patient anticipation that drove me wild. Those men and women gazing on us so stonily knew my companion's rank and faith. They had watched him riding in and out daily, one of the sights of their street, gay and gallant; and now with the same eyes they were watching greedily for the butchers to come. The very children took a fresh interest in him, as one doomed and dying; and waited panting for the show to begin. So I read them.

"Knock!" I repeated, angrily, losing all pa-

tience. Had I been foolish in bringing him back
to this part of the town where every soul knew
him? "Knock; we must get in, whether or no.
They can not all have left the house!"

I kicked the door desperately, and my relief
was great when it opened. A servant with a pale
face stood before me, his knees visibly shaking.
And behind him was Croisette.

I think we fell straightway into one another's
arms.

"And Marie," I cried, "Marie!"

"Marie is within, and madame," he answered,
joyfully; "we are together again and nothing
matters. But oh, Anne, where have you been?
And what is the matter? Is it a great fire? Or is
the king dead? Or what is it?"

I told him. I hastily poured out some of the
things which had happened to me, and some which
I feared were in store for others. Naturally he
was surprised and shocked by the latter, though
his fears had already been aroused. But his joy
and relief, when he heard the mystery of Louis de
Pavannes' marriage explained, were so great that
they swallowed up all other feelings. He could
not say enough about it. He pictured Louis again
and again as Kit's lover, as our old friend, our
companion; as true, stanch, brave without fear,
without reproach; and it was long before his eyes
ceased to sparkle, his tongue to run merrily, the

color to mantle in his cheeks—long, that is, as time is counted by minutes. But presently the remembrance of Louis' danger and our own position returned more vividly. Our plan for rescuing him had failed—failed!

"No! no!" cried Croisette, stoutly. He would not hear of it. He would not have it at any price. "No, we will not give up hope! We will go shoulder to shoulder and find him. Louis is as brave as a lion and as quick as a weasel. We will find him in time yet. We will go when — I mean as soon as —"

He faltered and paused. His sudden silence, as he looked round the empty forecourt in which we stood, was eloquent. The cold light, faint and uncertain yet, was stealing into the court, disclosing a row of stables on either side, and a tiny porter's hutch by the gates, and fronting us a noble house of four stories, tall, gray, grim-looking.

I assented; gloomily, however. "Yes," I said, "we will go when —"

And, I too, stopped. The same thought was in my mind. How could we leave these people? How could we leave madame in her danger and distress? How could we return her kindness by desertion? We could not. No, not for Kit's sake. Because after all Louis, our Louis, was a man, and must take his chance. He must take his chance. But I groaned.

So that was settled. I had already explained our plan to Croisette; and now, as we waited, he began to tell me a story, a long, confused story, about Madame d'O. I thought he was talking for the sake of talking — to keep up our spirits — and I did not attend much to him; so that he had not reached the gist of it, or at least I had not grasped it, when a noise without stayed his tongue. It was the tramp of footsteps, apparently of a large party in the street. It forced him to break off, and promptly drove us all to our posts.

But before we separated a slight figure, hardly noticeable in that dim, uncertain light, passed me quickly, laying for an instant a soft hand in mine as I stood waiting by the gates. I have said I scarcely saw the figure, though I did see the kind, timid eyes, and the pale cheeks under the hood; but I bent over the hand and kissed it, and felt, truth to tell, no more regret nor doubt where our duty lay. But stood, waiting patiently.

CHAPTER IX.

THE HEAD OF ERASMUS.

WAITING, and waiting alone! The gates were almost down now. The gang of ruffians without, reinforced each moment by volunteers eager for plunder, rained blows unceasingly on hinge and socket; and still hotter and faster through a dozen rifts in the timbers came the fire of their threats and curses. Many grew tired, but others replaced them. Tools broke, but they brought more and worked with savage energy. They had shown at first a measure of prudence, looking to be fired on, and to be resisted by men surprised, indeed, but desperate; and the bolder of them only had advanced. But now they pressed round unchecked, meeting no resistance. They would scarcely stand back to let the sledges have swing; but hallooed and ran in on the creaking beams and beat them with their fists whenever the gates swayed under a blow.

One stout iron bar still held its place. And this I watched as if fascinated. I was alone in the empty courtyard, standing a little aside, sheltered by one of the stone pillars from which the gates hung. Behind me the door of the house stood ajar. Candles, which the daylight rendered garish, still burned in the rooms on the first floor, of which the tall narrow windows were open. On the wide stone sill of one of these stood Croisette, a boyish figure, looking silently down at me, his hand on the latticed shutter. He looked pale, and I nodded and smiled at him. I felt rather anger than fear myself; remembering, as the fiendish cries half-deafened me, old tales of the Jacquerie and its doings, and how we had trodden it out.

Suddenly the din and tumult flashed to a louder note; as when hounds on the scent give tongue at sight. I turned quickly from the house, recalled to a sense of the position and peril. The iron bar was yielding to the pressure. Slowly the left wing of the gate was sinking inward. Through the widening chasm I caught a glimpse of wild, grimy faces and bloodshot eyes, and heard above the noise a sharp cry from Croisette, a cry of terror. Then I turned and ran, with a defiant gesture and an answering yell, right across the forecourt and up the steps to the door.

I ran the faster for the sharp report of a pistol behind me, and the whirr of a ball past my ear. But I was not scared by it, and as my feet alighted with a bound on the topmost step, I glanced back. The dogs were half-way across the court. I made a bungling attempt to shut and lock the great door—failed in this; and

heard behind me a roar of coarse triumph. I
waited for no more. I darted up the oak staircase four steps at a time, and rushed into the
great drawing-room on my left, banging the door
behind me.

The once splendid room was in a state of strange
disorder. Some of the rich tapestry had been
hastily torn down. One window was closed and
shuttered; no doubt Croisette had done it. The
other two were open, as if there had not been time
to close them, and the cold light which they
admitted contrasted in ghastly fashion with the
yellow rays of candles still burning in the sconces.
The furniture had been huddled aside or piled
into a barricade, a *chevaux de frise* of chairs and
tables stretching across the width of the room,
its interstices stuffed with, and its weakness
partly screened by, the torn-down hangings.
Behind this frail defense their backs to a door
which seemed to lead to an inner room, stood
Marie and Croisette, pale and defiant. The former had a long pike; the latter leveled a heavy,
bell-mouthed arquebuse across the back of a
chair, and blew up his match as I entered. Both
had in addition procured swords. I darted like
a rabbit through a little tunnel left on purpose for
me in the rampart, and took my stand by them.

"Is all right?" ejaculated Croisette, turning to
me nervously.

"All right, I think," I answered. I was breath-less.

"You are not hurt?"

"Not touched!"

I had just time then to draw my sword before the assailants streamed into the room, a dozen ruffians, reeking and tattered, with flushed faces and greedy, staring eyes. Once inside, however, suddenly — so suddenly that an idle spectator might have found the change ludicrous — they came to a stop. Their wild cries ceased, and tumbling over one another with curses and oaths they halted, surveying us in muddled surprise; seeing what was before them, and not liking it. Their leader appeared to be a tall butcher, with a pole-axe on his half-naked shoulder, but there were among them two or three soldiers in the royal livery and carrying pikes. They had looked for victims only, having met with no resistance at the gate, and the foremost recoiled now on find-ing themselves confronted by the muzzle of the arquebuse and the lighted match.

I seized the occasion. I knew, indeed, that the pause presented our only chance, and I sprang on a chair and waved my hand for silence. The instinct of obedience for the moment asserted itself; there was a stillness in the room.

"Beware!" I cried, loudly — as loudly and con-fidently as I could, considering that there was a

quaver at my heart as I looked on those savage
faces, which met and yet avoided my eye. "Beware of what you do! We are Catholics one and
all like yourselves, and good sons of the church.
Ay, and good subjects, too! *Vive le roi*, gentlemen! God save the king! I say." And I struck
the barricade with my sword until the metal rang
again. "God save the king!"

"Cry *Vive la Messe!*" shouted one.

"Certainly, gentlemen!" I replied, with politeness. "With all my heart. *Vive la Messe! Vive
la Messe!*"

This took the butcher, who luckily was still
sober, utterly aback. He had never thought of
this. He stared at us as if the ox he had been
about to fell had opened his mouth and spoken,
and, grievously at a loss, he looked for help to his
companions.

Later in the day, some Catholics were killed by
the mob. But their deaths, as far as could be
learned afterward, were due to private feuds. Save
in such cases—and they were few—the cry of
Vive la Messe! always obtained at least a respite;
more easily of course in the earlier hours of the
morning when the mob were scarce at ease in their
liberty to kill, while killing still seemed murder,
and men were not yet drunk with bloodshed.

I read the hesitation of the gang in their faces,
and when one asked roughly who we were, I

replied with greater boldness, "I am M. Anne de Caylus, nephew to the Vicomte de Caylus, governor, under the king, of Bayonne and the Landes!" This I said with what majesty I could. "And these," I continued, "are my brothers. You will harm us at your peril, gentlemen. The vicomte, believe me, will avenge every hair of our heads."

I can shut my eyes now and see the stupid wonder, the balked ferocity, of those gaping faces. Dull and savage as the men were, they were impressed; they saw reason indeed, and all seemed going well for us when some one in the rear shouted, "Cursed whelps! Throw them over!"

I looked swiftly in the direction whence the voice came — the darkest corner of the room — the corner by the shuttered window. I thought I made out a slender figure, cloaked and masked, a woman's it might be but I could not be certain, and beside it a couple of sturdy fellows, who kept apart from the herd and well behind their fugelman.

The speaker's courage arose no doubt from his position at the back of the room, for the foremost of the assailants seemed less determined. We were only three, and we must have gone down, barricade and all, before a rush. But three are three. And an arquebuse — Croisette's match burned splendidly — well loaded with slugs is an ugly weapon

at five paces, and makes nasty wounds, besides
scattering its charge famously. This a good many
of them, and the leaders in particular, seemed to
recognize. We might certainly take two or three
lives, and life is valuable to its owner when plunder is afoot. Besides most of them had common
sense enough to remember that there were scores
of Huguenots, genuine heretics, to be robbed
for the killing; so why go out of the way, they
reasoned, to cut a Catholic throat and perhaps
get into trouble? Why risk Montfaucon for a
whim, and offend a man of influence like the
Vicomte de Caylus for nothing?

Unfortunately at this crisis their original design
was recalled to their minds by the same voice
behind crying out, "Pavannes! Where is
Pavannes?"

"Ay!" shouted the butcher, grasping the idea
and at the same time spitting on his hands and
taking a fresh grip of the ax, "Show us the
heretic dog, and go! Let us at him."

"M. de Pavannes," I said, coolly — but I could
not take my eyes off the shining blade of that
man's ax, it was so very broad and sharp — "is
not here!"

"That is a lie! He is in that room behind
you!" the prudent gentleman in the background
called out. "Give him up!"

"Ay, give him up!" echoed the **man of the**

pole-ax almost good-humoredly, "or it will be the worse for you. Let us have at him and get you gone!"

This with an air of much reason, while a growl as of a chained beast ran through the crowd, mingled with cries of "*A mort les Huguenots! Vive Lorraine!*" — cries which seemed to show that all did not approve of the indulgence offered us.

"Beware, gentlemen, beware," I urged; "I swear he is not here! I swear it; do you hear?"

A howl of impatience and then a sudden movement of the crowd as though the rush were coming, warned me to temporize no longer. "Stay! Stay!" I added, hastily. "One minute! Hear me! You are too many for us. Will you swear to let us go safe and untouched if we give you passage?"

A dozen voices shrieked assent. But I looked at the butcher only. He seemed to be an honest man out of his profession.

"Ay, I swear it!" he cried, with a nod.

"By the mass?"

"By the mass."

I twitched Croisette's sleeve, and he tore the fuse from his weapon and flung the gun — too heavy to be of use to us longer — to the ground. It was done in a moment. While the mob swept over the barricade and smashed the rich furniture of it in wanton malice, we filed aside and nimbly slipped under it one by one. Then we hurried in single file to the end of the room, no one taking much notice of us. All were pressing on, intent on their prey. We gained the door as the butcher struck his first blow on that which we had guarded — on that which we had given up. We sprang down the stairs with bounding hearts, heard as we reached the outer door the roar of many voices, but stayed not to look behind — paused indeed for nothing. Fear, to speak candidly, lent us wings. In three seconds we had leaped the prostrate gates and were in the street. A cripple, two or three dogs, a knot of women looking timidly yet curiously in, a horse tethered to the staple — we saw nothing else. No one stayed us. No one raised a hand, and in another minute we had turned a corner and were out of sight of the house.

"They will take a gentleman's word another time," I said, with a quiet smile, as I put up my sword.

"I would like to see her face at this moment," Croisette replied. "You saw Madame d'O?"

I shook my head, not answering. I was not sure, and I had a queer, sickening dread of the subject. If I had seen her, I had seen — oh! it was too horrible, too unnatural! Her own sister! Her own brother-in-law.

I hastened to change the subject. "The Pavannes," I made shift to say, "must have had five minutes' start."

"More," Croisette answered, "if madame and he got away at once. If all has gone well with them, and they have not been stopped in the streets they should be at Mirepoix's by now. They seemed to be pretty sure that he would take them in."

"Ah!" I sighed. "What fools we were to bring madame from that place! If we had not meddled with her affairs we might have reached Louis long ago — our Louis, I mean."

"True," Croisette answered softly, "but remember that then we should not have saved the other Louis, as I trust we have. He would still be in Pallavicini's hands. Come, Anne, let us think it is all for the best," he added, his face shining with a steady courage that shamed me. "To the rescue! Heaven will help us to be in time yet!"

"Ay, to the rescue!" I replied, catching his spirit. "First to the right, I think, second to the left, first on the right again. That was the direction given us, was it not? The house opposite a book-shop with the sign of the Head of Erasmus. Forward, boys! We may do it yet."

But before I pursue our fortunes farther let me explain. The room we had guarded so jealously was empty! The plan had been mine and I was proud of it. For once Croisette had fallen into his rightful place. My flight from the gate, the vain attempt to close the house, the barricade before the inner door — these were all designed to draw the assailants to one spot. Pavannes and his wife — the latter hastily disguised as a boy — had hidden behind the door of the hutch by the gates — the porter's hutch, and had slipped out and fled in the first confusion of the attack.

Even the servants, as we learned afterward, who had hidden themselves in the lower parts of the house, got away in the same manner, though some of them — they were but few in all — were stopped as Huguenots and killed before the day ended. I had the more reason to hope that Pavannes and his wife would get clear off, inasmuch as I had given the duke's ring to him, thinking it might serve him in a strait, and believing that we should have little to fear ourselves, once clear of his house, unless we should meet the vidame indeed.

We did not meet him as it turned out, but before we had traversed a quarter of the distance we had to go we found that fears based on reason were not the only terrors we had to resist. Pavannes' house, where we had hitherto been, stood at some distance from the center of the blood-storm which was enwrapping unhappy

Paris that morning. It was several hundred paces from the Rue de Bethisy where the admiral lived, and what with this comparative remoteness and the excitement of our own little drama, we had not attended much to the fury of the bells, the shots and cries and uproar which proclaimed the state of the city. We had not pictured the scenes which were happening so near. Now in the streets the truth broke upon us, and drove the blood from our cheeks. A hundred yards, the turning of a corner, sufficed. We who but yesterday left the country, who only a week before were boys, careless as other boys, not reck-ing of death at all, were plunged now into the midst of horrors I can not describe. And the awful contrast between the sky above and the things about us! Even now the lark was singing not far from us; the sunshine was striking the topmost stories of the houses; the fleecy clouds were passing overhead, the freshness of a summer morning was—

Ah! where was it? Not here in the narrow lanes surely, that echoed and re-echoed with shrieks and curses and frantic prayers; in which bands of furious men rushed up and down, and where archers of the guard and the more cruel rabble were breaking in doors and windows, and hurry-ing with bloody weapons from house to house, seeking, pursuing, and at last killing in some

12

horrid corner, some place of darkness — killing
with blow on blow dealt on writhing bodies! Not
here, surely, where each minute a child, a woman
died silently, a man snarling like a wolf — happy
if he had snatched his weapon and got his back
to the wall; where foul corpses dammed the very
blood that ran down the kennel, and children —
little children — played with them!

I was at Cahors in 1580 in the great street fight;
and there women were killed. I was with Chatil-
lon nine years later, when he rode through the
Faubourgs of Paris, with this very day and his
father Coligny in his mind, and gave no quarter.
I was at Courtas and Ivry, and more than once
have seen prisoners led out to be piked in batches
— ay, and by hundreds! But war is war, and
these were its victims, dying for the most part
under God's heaven with arms in their hands;
not men and women fresh roused from their
sleep. I felt on those occasions no such horror,
I have never felt such burning pity and indignation as on the morning I am describing, that
long-passed summer morning when I first saw the
sun shining on the streets of Paris. Croisette
clung to me, sick and white, shutting his eyes
and ears, and letting me guide him as I would.
Marie strode along on the other side of him, his
lips closed, his eyes sinister. Once a soldier of
the guard whose blood-stained hands betrayed

the work he had done, came reeling — he was
drunk, as were many of the butchers — across
our path, and I gave way a little. Marie did not,
but walked stolidly on as if he did not see him,
as if the way were clear, and there were no ugly
thing in God's image blocking it.

Only his hand went as if by accident to the
haft of his dagger. The archer — fortunately for
himself and for us, too — reeled clear of us. We
escaped that danger. But to see women killed
and pass by — it was horrible! So horrible that
if in those moments I had had the wishing-cap, I
would have asked but for five thousand riders,
and leave to charge with them through the streets
of Paris! I would have had the days of the
Jacquerie back again, and my men-at-arms
behind me!

For ourselves, though the orgy was at its height
when we passed, we were not molested. We were
stopped indeed three times — once in each of the
streets we traversed — by different bands of
murderers. But as we wore the same badges
as themselves, and cried "*Vive la Messe!*" and
gave our names, we were allowed to proceed. I
can give no idea of the confusion and uproar, and
I scarcely believe myself now that we saw some
of the things we witnessed. Once a man gaily
dressed, and splendidly mounted, dashed past us,
waving his naked sword and crying in a frenzied

way, "Bleed them! Bleed them! Bleed in May,
as good to-day!" and never ceased crying out the
same words until he passed beyond our hearing.
Once we came upon the bodies of a father and two
sons, which lay piled together in the kennel;
partly stripped already. The youngest boy could
not have been more than thirteen. I mention this
group, not as surpassing others in pathos, but
because it is well known now that this boy,
Jacques Nompar de Caumont, was not dead, but
lives to-day, my friend the Marshal de la Force.

This reminds me, too, of the single act of kindness we were able to perform. We found ourselves suddenly, on turning a corner, amid a gang
of seven or eight soldiers, who had stopped and
surrounded a handsome boy, apparently about
fourteen. He wore a scholar's gown, and had
some books under his arm, to which he clung
firmly — though only perhaps by instinct — not-
withstanding the furious air of the men who were
threatening him with death. They were loudly
demanding his name as we paused opposite them.
He either could not or would not give it, but said
several times in his fright that he was going to
the College of Burgundy. Was he a Catholic?
they cried. He was silent. With an oath the
man who had hold of his collar lifted up his pike,
and naturally the lad raised the books to guard
his face. A cry broke from Croisette. He rushed
forward to stay the blow.

"See! see!" he exclaimed, loudly, his voice arresting the man's arm in the very act of falling. "He has a Mass Book! He has a Mass Book! He is not a heretic! He is a Catholic!"

The fellow lowered his weapon, and sullenly snatched the books. He looked at them stupidly with bloodshot wandering eyes, the red cross on the vellum bindings the only thing he understood. But it was enough for him; he bid the boy begone and released him with a cuff and an oath.

Croisette was not satisfied with this, though I did not understand his reason; only I saw him exchange a glance with the lad. "Come, come!" he said, lightly. "Give him his books! You do not want them!"

But on that the men turned savagely upon us. They did not thank us for the part we had already taken; and this they thought was going too far. They were half-drunk and quarrelsome, and being two to one, and two over, began to flourish their weapons in our faces. Mischief would certainly have been done, and very quickly, had not an unexpected ally appeared on our side.

"Put up! put up!" this gentleman cried in a boisterous voice — he was already in our midst. "What is all this about? What is the use of fighting among ourselves, when there is many a bonny throat to cut, and heaven to be gained by it! Put up, I say!"

"Who are you?" they roared in chorus.

"The Duke of Guise!" he answered, coolly. "Let the gentlemen go, and be hanged to you, you rascals!"

The man's bearing was a stronger argument than his words, for I am sure that a stouter or more reckless blade never swaggered in church or street. I knew him instantly, and even the crew of butchers seemed to see in him their master. They flung back a few curses at him, but having nothing to gain they yielded. They threw down the books with contempt — showing thereby their sense of true religion; and trooped off roaring, "*Tuez! Tuez!* Aux Huguenots!" at the top of their voices.

The newcomer thus left with us was Buré — Blaise Buré — the same who only yesterday, though it seemed months and months back, had lured us into Bezers' power. Since that moment we had not seen him. Now he had wiped off part of the debt, and we looked at him, uncertain whether to reproach him or not. He, however, was not one whit abashed, but returned our regards with a not unkindly leer.

"I bear no malice, young gentlemen," he said, impudently.

"No, I should think not," I answered.

"And besides, we are quits now," the knave continued.

"You are very kind," I said.

"To be sure. You did me a good turn once," he answered, much to my surprise. He seemed to be in earnest now. "You do not remember it, young gentleman, but it was you and your brother here," he pointed to Croisette, "did it! And by the Pope and the King of Spain I have not forgotten it!"

"I have," I said.

"What! You have forgotten spitting that fellow at Caylus ten days ago? *Ca! sa!* You remember. And very cleanly done, too! A pretty stroke! Well, M. Anne, that was a clever fellow, a very clever fellow. He thought so, and I thought so, and what was more to the purpose the most noble Raoul de Bezers thought so too. You understand?"

He leered at me and I did understand. I understood that unwittingly I had rid Blaise Buré of a rival. This accounted for the respectful, almost the kindly, way in which he had — well, deceived us.

"That is all," he said. "If you want as much done for you, let me know. For the present, gentlemen, farewell!"

He cocked his hat fiercely, and went off at speed the way we had ourselves been going, humming as he went,

" Ce petit homme tant joli,
Qui toujours cause et toujours rit,
Qui toujours baise sa mignonne
Dieu gard' de mal ce petit homme!"

His reckless song came back to us on the summer breeze. We watched him make a playful pass at a corpse which some one had propped in ghastly fashion against a door, and miss it, and go on whistling the same air, and then a corner hid him from view.

We lingered only a moment ourselves, merely to speak to the boy we had befriended.

"Show the books if any one challenges you," said Croisette to him, shrewdly. Croisette was so much of a boy himself, with his fair hair like a halo about his white, excited face, that the picture of the two, one advising the other, seemed to me a strangely pretty one. "Show the books and point to the cross on them. And heaven send you safe to your college."

"I would like to know your name, if you please," said the boy. His coolness and dignity struck me as admirable under the circumstances. "I am Maximilian de Bethune, son of the Baron de Rosny."

"Then," said Croisette, briskly, "one good turn has deserved another. Your father yesterday at Etampes — no it was the day before, but we have not been in bed — warned us — "

He broke off suddenly; then cried, "Run! run!"

The boy needed no second warning indeed. He was off like the wind down the street, for we had seen, and so had he, the stealthy approach of two or three prowling rascals on the look-out for a victim. They caught sight of him and were strongly inclined to follow him, but we were their match in numbers. The street was otherwise empty at the moment, and we showed them three excellent reasons why they should give him a clear start.

His after-adventures are well known, for he, too, lives. He was stopped twice after he left us. In each case he escaped by showing his book of offices. On reaching the college the porter refused to admit him, and he remained for some time in the open street exposed to constant danger of losing his life, and knowing not what to do. At length he induced the gatekeeper, by the present of some small pieces of money, to call the principal of the college, and this man humanely concealed him for three days. The massacre being then at an end, two armed men in his father's pay sought him out and restored him to his friends. So near was France to losing her greatest minister, the Duke de Sully.

To return to ourselves. The lad out of sight, we instantly resumed our purpose, and trying to shut our eyes and ears to the cruelty, and ribaldry,

and uproar through which we had still to pass,
we counted our turnings with a desperate exact-
ness, intent only on one thing — to reach Louis de
Pavannes, to reach the house opposite to the Head
of Erasmus, as quickly as we could. We presently
entered a long, narrow street. At the end of it
the river was visible, gleaming and sparkling in
the sunlight. The street was quiet; quiet and
empty. There was no living soul to be seen
from end to end of it, only a prowling dog. The
noise of the tumult raging in other parts was
softened here by distance and the intervening
houses. We seemed to be able to breathe more
freely.

"This should be our street," said Croisette.

I nodded. At the same moment I espied, half-
way down it, the sign we needed and pointed to it.
But ah! were we in time? Or too late? That
was the question. By a single impulse we broke
into a run, and shot down the roadway at speed.
A few yards short of the Head of Erasmus we
came, one by one, Croisette first, to a full stop.
A full stop!

The house opposite the bookseller's was sacked;
gutted from top to bottom. It was a tall house,
immediately fronting the street, and every window
in it was broken. The door hung forlornly on
one hinge, glaring cracks in its surface showing
where the ax had splintered it. Fragments of

glass and ware, flung out and shattered in sheer
wantonness, strewed the steps; and down one corner of the latter a dark red stream trickled — to
curdle by and by in the gutter.   Whence came
the stream?   Alas! there was something more to
be seen yet; something our eyes instinctively
sought last of all.   The body of a man.

It lay on the threshold, the head hanging back,
the wide, glazed eyes looking up to the summer
sky whence the sweltering heat would soon pour
down upon it.   We looked shuddering at the face.
It was that of a servant, a valet who had been
with Louis at Caylus.   We recognized him at
once, for we had known and liked him.   He had
carried our guns on the hills a dozen times, and
told us stories of the war.   The blood crawled
slowly from him.   He was dead.

Croisette began to shake all over.   He clutched
one of the pillars which bore up the porch, and
pressed his face against its cold surface, hiding
his eyes from the sight.   The worst had come.
In our hearts I think we had always fancied some
accident would save *our* friend, some stranger
warn him.

"Oh, poor, poor Kit!" Croisette cried, bursting
suddenly into violent sobs.   "Oh, Kit! Kit!"

CHAPTER X.

HAU, HAU, HUGUENOTS!

His late majesty Henry the IV, I remember, than whom no braver man wore sword, who loved danger indeed for its own sake, and courted it as a mistress, could never sleep on the night before an action. I have heard him say himself that it was so before the fight at Arques. Croisette partook of this nature too, being high-strung and apt to be easily overwrought, but never until the necessity for exertion had passed away; while Marie and I, though not a whit stouter at a pinch, were slower to feel and less easy to move — more Germanic in fact.

I name this here partly lest it should be thought after what I have just told of Croisette that there was anything of the woman about him — save the tenderness; and partly to show that we acted at this crisis each after his manner. While Croisette turned pale and trembled, and hid his eyes, I stood dazed, looking from the desolate house to the face stiffening in the sunshine, and back again; wondering, though I had seen scores of dead faces since daybreak, and a plenitude of suffering in all dreadful shapes, how Providence could let this happen to us. To us! In his instincts man is as selfish as any animal that lives.

I saw nothing indeed of the dead face and dead house after the first convincing glance. I saw, instead, with hot, hot eyes the old castle at home, the green fields about the brook, and the gray hills rising from them; and the terrace, and Kit coming to meet us, Kit with white face and parted lips and avid eyes that questioned us! And we with no comfort to give her, no lover to bring back to her!

A faint noise behind as of a sign creaking in the wind, roused me from this most painful reverie. I turned round, not quickly or in surprise or fear. Rather in the same dull wonder. The upper part of the bookseller's door was ajar. It was that I had heard opened. An old woman was peering out at us.

As our eyes met, she made a slight movement to close the door again. But I did not stir, and seeming to be reassured by a second glance, she nodded to me in a stealthy fashion. I drew a step nearer, listlessly. "Pst! Pst!" she whispered. Her wrinkled old face, which was like a Normandy apple long kept, was soft with pity as she looked at Croisette. "Pst!"

"Well!" I said, mechanically.

"Is he taken?" she muttered.

"Who taken?" I asked, stupidly.

She nodded toward the forsaken house, and answered, "The young lord who lodged there? Ah! sirs," she continued, "he looked gay and handsome, if you'll believe me, as he came from the king's court yester even. As bonny a sight in his satin coat and his ribbons as my eyes ever saw. And to think that they should be hunting him like a rat to-day!"

The woman's words were few and simple; but what a change they made in my world. How my heart awoke from its stupor and leaped up with a new joy and a new-born hope? "Did he get away?" I cried, eagerly. "Did he escape, mother, then?"

"Ay, that he did!" she replied, quickly. "That poor fellow yonder—he lies quiet enough now. God forgive him his heresy, say I—kept the door manfully while the gentleman got on the roof and ran right down the street on the tops of the houses, with them firing and hooting at him, for all the world as if he had been a squirrel and they a pack of boys with stones!"

"And he escaped?"

"Escaped!" she answered more slowly, shaking her old head in doubt. "I do not know about that. I fear that they have got him by now, gentlemen. I have been shivering and shaking up-stairs with my husband—he is in bed, good man, and the safest place for him—the saints have mercy upon us!   But I heard them go with their shouting and gunpowder right along to the river, and I doubt they will take him between this and the *Châtelet!*   I doubt they will."

"How long ago was it, dame?" I cried.

"Oh! may be half an hour.   Perhaps you are friends of his?" she added, questioningly.

But I did not stay to answer her.   I shook Croisette, who had not heard a word of this, by the shoulder.   "There is a chance that he has escaped!" I cried in his ear.   "Escaped, do you hear?"   And I told him hastily what she had said.

It was fine, indeed, and a sight to see the blood rush to his cheeks, and the tears dry in his eyes, and energy and decision spring to life in every nerve and muscle of his face.   "Then there is hope?" he cried, grasping my arm.   "Hope, Anne! Come! Come! Do not let us lose another instant.   If he be alive let us join him!"

The old woman tried to detain us, but in vain. Nay, pitying us, and fearing, I think, that we were rushing on our deaths, she cast aside her caution, and called after us aloud.   We took no heed, running after Croisette, who had not waited for our answer, as fast as young limbs could carry us down the street.   The exhaustion we had felt a moment before when all seemed lost — be it remembered that we had not been to bed or tasted food for many hours — fell from us on the instant, and was clean gone and forgotten in the joy of this respite. Louis was living, and for the moment had escaped.

Escaped! But for how long? We soon had our answer. The moment we turned the corner by the riverside, the murmur of a multitude not loud but continuous, struck our ears, even as the breeze off the water swept our cheeks. Across the river lay the thousand roofs of the Ile de la Cité, all sparkling in the sunshine. But we swept to the right, thinking little of *that* sight, and checked our speed on finding ourselves on the skirts of the crowd. Before us was a bridge — the Pont au Change, I think — and at its head on our side of the water stood the *Châtelet*, with its hoary turrets and battlements. Between us and the latter, and backed only by the river, was a great open space half-filled with people, mostly silent and watchful, come together as to a show, and betraying, at present at least, no desire to take an active part in what was going on.

We hurriedly plunged into the throng, and soon caught the clue to the quietness and the lack of movement which seemed to prevail, and which at first sight had puzzled us. For a moment the absence of the dreadful symptoms we had come to know so well — the flying and pursuing, the random blows, the shrieks and curses, and batterings on doors, the tipsy yells, had reassured us. But the relief was short-lived. The people before us were under control. A tighter grip seemed to close upon our hearts as we discerned this, for we knew that the wild fury of the populace, like the rush of a bull, might have given some chance of escape — in this case as in others. But this cold-blooded ordered search left none.

Every face about us was turned in the same direction, away from the river and toward a block of old houses which stood opposite to it. The space immediately in front of these was empty, the people being kept back by a score or so of archers of the guard set at intervals, and by as many horsemen, who kept riding up and down, belaboring the bolder spirits with the flat of their swords, and so preserving a line. At each extremity of this — more noticeably on our left where the line curved round the angle of the buildings — stood a handful of riders, seven in a group perhaps. And alone in the middle of the space so kept clear, walking his horse up and down and gazing at the houses, rode a man of great stature, booted and armed, the feather nodding in his bonnet. I could not see his face, but I had no need to see it. I knew him, and groaned aloud. It was Bezers!

I understood the scene better now. The horse-

men, stern, bearded Switzers for the most part,
who eyed the rabble about them with grim disdain,
and were by no means chary of their blows, were
all in his colors and armed to the teeth. The
order and discipline were of his making, the
revenge of his seeking. A grasp as of steel had
settled upon our friend, and I felt that his last
chance was gone. Louis de Pavannes might as
well be lying on his threshold with his dead
servant by his side, as be in hiding within that
ring of ordered swords.

It was with despairing eyes we looked at the
old wooden houses. They seemed to be bowing
themselves toward us, their upper stories pro-
jected so far, they were so decrepit. Their roofs
were a wilderness of gutters and crooked gables,
of tottering chimneys and wooden pinnacles and
rotting beams. Among these I judged Kit's
lover was hiding. Well, it was a good place for
hide and seek—with any other player than *Death.*
In the ground floors of the houses there were no
windows and no doors; by reason, I learned afterward, of the frequent flooding of the river. But
a long wooden gallery raised on struts ran along
the front, rather more than the height of a man
from the ground, and access to this was gained by
a wooden staircase at each end. Above this first
gallery was a second, and above that a line of
windows set between the gables. The block—it

may have run for seventy or eighty yards along
the shore — contained four houses, each with a
door opening on to the lower gallery. I saw indeed
that but for the vidame's precautions Louis might
well have escaped. Had the mob once poured
helter-skelter into that labyrinth of rooms and
passages he might with luck have mingled with
them, unheeded and unrecognized, and effected
his escape when they retreated.

But now there were sentries on each gallery and
more on the roof. Whenever one of the latter
moved or seemed to be looking inward — where a
search party, I understood, were at work— indeed,
if he did but turn his head, a thrill ran through the
crowd and a murmur arose, which once or twice
swelled to a savage roar, such as earlier had made
me tremble. When this happened the impulse
came, it seemed to me, from the farther end of
the line. There the rougher elements were collected, and there I more than once saw Bezers'
troopers in conflict with the mob. In that quarter, too, a savage chant was presently struck up,
the whole gathering joining in and yelling with
an indescribably appalling effect:

> "Hau! Hau! Huguenots!
> Faites place aux Papegots!"

In derision of the old song said to be popular
among the Protestants. But in the Huguenot
version the last words were, of course, transposed,

We had worked our way by this time to the
front of the line, and, looking into one another's
eyes, mutely asked a question; but not even Croisette had an answer ready. There could be no
answer but one. What could we do? Nothing.
We were too late. Too late again! And yet how
dreadful it was to stand still among the cruel,
thoughtless mob and see our friend, the touch of
whose hand we knew so well, done to death for
their sport! Done to death, as the old woman had
said, like any rat, not a soul save ourselves pitying him! Not a soul to turn sick at his cry of
agony, or shudder at the glance of his dying eyes.
It was dreadful indeed.

"Ah, well," muttered a woman beside me to
her companion — there were many women in the
crowd —"it is down with the Huguenots, say I.
It is Lorraine is the fine man! But after all yon
is a bonny fellow and a proper, Margot! I saw
him leap from roof to roof over Love Lane, as if
the blessed saints had carried him. And him a
heretic!"

"It is the black art," the other answered, crossing herself.

"May be it is! But he will need it all to give
that big man the slip to-day," replied the first
speaker comfortably.

"That devil!" Margot exclaimed, pointing
with a stealthy gesture of hate at the vidame,

And then in a fierce whisper, with inarticulate threats, she told a story of him, which made me shudder. "He did! And she in religion too!" she concluded. "May our Lady of Loretto reward him."

The tale might be true for aught I knew, horrible as it was. I had heard similar ones attributing things almost as fiendish to him, times and again; from that poor fellow lying dead on Pavannes' doorstep for one, and from others besides. As the vidame in his pacing to and fro turned toward us, I gazed at him, fascinated by his grim visage and that story. His eye rested on the crowd about us, and I trembled, lest even at that distance he should recognize us.

And he did! I had forgotten his keenness of sight. His face flashed suddenly into a grim smile. The tail of his eye resting upon us, and seeming to forbid us to move, he gave some orders. The color fled from my face. To escape indeed was impossible, for we were hemmed in by the press, and could scarcely stir a limb. Yet I did make one effort.

"Croisette!" I muttered — he was the rearmost — "stoop down. He may not have seen you. Stoop down, lad!"

But St. Croix was obstinate and would not stoop. Nay, when one of the mounted men came, and roughly ordered us into the open, it was

Croisette who pushing past us stepped out first with a lordly air. I, following him, saw that his lips were firmly compressed and that there was an eager light in his eyes. As we emerged, the crowd in our wake broke the line, and tried to pursue us, either hostilely or through eagerness to see what it meant. But a dozen blows of the long pikes drove them back, howling and cursing to their places.

I expected to be taken to Bezers, and what would follow I could not tell. But he did always it seemed what we least expected, for he only scowled at us now, a grim mockery on his lips, and cried, "See that they do not escape again! But do them no harm, sirrah, until I have the batch of them!"

He turned one way and I another, my heart swelling with rage. Would he dare to harm us? Would even the vidame dare to murder a Caylus' nephew openly and in cold blood? I did not think so. And yet — and yet —

Croisette interrupted the train of my thoughts. I found that he was not following me. He had sprung away, and in a dozen strides reached the vidame's stirrup, and was clasping his knee when I turned. I could not hear at the distance at which I stood, what he said, and the horseman to whom Bezers had committed us spurred between us. But I heard the vidame's answer.

"No! no! no!" he cried, with a ring of restrained fury in his voice. "Let my plans alone! What do you know of them? And if you speak to me again, M. St. Croix — I think that is your name, boy — I will — no, I will not kill you. That might please you; you are stubborn, I can see. But I will have you stripped and lashed like the meanest of my scullions! Now go, and take care!"

Impatience, hate and wild passion flamed in his face for the moment, transfiguring it. Croisette came back to us slowly, white-lipped and quiet. "Never mind," I said, bitterly. "The third time may bring luck."

Not that I felt much indignation at the vidame's insult, or any anger with the lad for incurring it, as I had felt on that other occasion. Life and death seemed to be everything on this morning. Words had ceased to please and annoy, for what are words to the sheep in the shambles? One man's life and one woman's happiness — outside ourselves we thought only of these now. And some day, I reflected, Croisette might remember, even with pleasure, that he had, as a drowning man clutching at straws, stooped to a last prayer for them.

We were placed in the middle of a knot of troopers who closed the line to the right. And presently Marie touched me. He was gazing

intently at the sentry on the roof of the third
house from us, the farthest but one. The man's
back was to the parapet, and he was gesticulating
wildly.

"He sees him!" Marie muttered.

I nodded almost in apathy. But this passed
away, and I started involuntarily and shuddered,
as a savage roar, breaking the silence, rang along
the front of the mob like a rolling volley of
firearms. What was it? A man posted at a window on the upper gallery had dropped his pike's
point, and was leveling it at some one inside; we
could see no more.

But those in front of the window could; they
saw too much for the vidame's precautions, as a
moment showed. He had not laid his account
with the frenzy of a rabble, the passions of a mob
which had tasted blood. I saw the line at its
farther end waver suddenly and toss to and fro.
Then a hundred hands went up, and confused
angry cries rose with them. The troopers struck
about them, giving back slowly as they did so.
But their efforts were in vain. With a scream of
triumph a wild torrent of people broke through
between them, leaving them stranded, and
rushed in a headlong cataract toward the steps.
Bezers was close to us at the time. "S'death!"
he cried, swearing oaths which even his sovereign
could scarce have equaled. "They will snatch
him from me yet, the hell-hounds!"

He whirled his horse around and spurred him
in a dozen bounds to the stairs at our end of the
gallery. There he leaped from him, dropping the
bridle recklessly; and bounding up three steps at
a time, he ran along the gallery. Half a dozen
of the troopers about us stayed only to fling their
reins to one of their number, and then followed,
their great boots clattering on the planks.

My breath came fast and short, for I felt it was
a crisis. It was a race between the two parties,
or rather between the vidame and the leaders of
the mob. The latter had the shorter way to go;
but on the narrow steps they were carried off
their feet by the press behind them, and fell over
and hampered one another, and lost time. The
vidame, free from this drawback, was some way
along the gallery before they had set foot on it.

How I prayed — amid a scene of the wildest
uproar and excitement — that the mob might be
first! Let there be only a short conflict between
Bezers' men and the people, and in the confusion
Pavannes might yet escape. Hope awoke in the
turmoil. Above the yells of the crowd a score of
deep voices about me thundered "A Wolf! A
Wolf!" And I too, lost my head, and drew my
sword, and screamed at the top of my voice, "A
Caylus! A Caylus!" with the maddest.

Thousands of eyes besides mine were strained
on the foremost figures on either side. They met

as it chanced precisely at the door of the house. The mob leader was a slender man, I saw; a priest apparently, though now he was girt with unpriestly weapons, his skirts were tucked up, and his head was bare. So much my first glance showed me. It was at the second look—it was when I saw the blood forsake his pale, lowering face and leave it whiter than ever, when horror sprang along with recognition to his eyes, when borne along by the crowd behind he saw his position and who was before him—it was only then when his mean figure shrank, and he quailed and would have turned but could not, that I recognized the coadjutor.

I was silent now, my mouth agape. There are seconds which are minutes; ay, and many minutes. A man may die, a man may come into life in such a second. In one of these, it seemed to me, those two men paused, face to face; though in fact a pause was for one of them impossible. He was between—and I think he knew it—the devil and the deep sea. Yet he seemed to pause, while all, even that yelling crowd below, held their breath. The next moment, glaring askance at one another like two dogs unevenly coupled, he and Bezers shot shoulder to shoulder into the doorway, and in another jot of time would have been out of sight. But then, in that instant, I saw something happen. The vidame's hand flashed up above the priest's head, and the cross-hilt of his sheathed sword crashed down with awful force, and still more awful passion, on the other's tonsure. The wretch went down like a log, without a word, without a cry. Amid a roar of rage from a thousand throats, a roar that might have shaken the stoutest heart and blanched the swarthiest cheek, Bezers disappeared within.

It was then I saw the power of discipline and custom. Few as were the troopers who had followed him — a mere handful — they fell without hesitation on the foremost of the crowd, who were already in confusion, stumbling and falling over their leader's body, and hurled them back pell-mell along the gallery. The throng below had no firearms, and could give no aid at the moment; the stage was narrow; in two minutes the vidame's people had swept it clear of the crowd and were in possession of it. A tall fellow took up the priest's body, dead or alive, I do not know which, and flung it as if it had been a sack of corn over the rail. It fell with a heavy thud on the ground. I heard a piercing scream that rose above that babel, one shrill scream, and the mob closed round and hid the thing.

If the rascals had had the wit to make at once for the right-hand stairs, where we stood with two or three of Bezers' men who had kept their saddles, I think they might easily have disposed of us, encumbered as we were, by the horses; and then they could have attacked the handful on the gallery on both flanks. But the mob had no leaders, and no plan of operations. They seized indeed two or three of the scattered troopers, and tearing them from their horses, wreaked their passion upon them horribly. But most of the Switzers escaped, thanks to the attention the mob paid to the houses and what was going forward on the galleries; and these, extricating themselves, joined us one by one, so that gradually a little ring of stern faces gathered about the stair-foot. A moment's hesitation, and seeing no help for it, we ranged ourselves with them; and, unchecked as unbidden, sprang on three of the led horses.

All this passed more quickly than I can relate it; so that before our feet were well in the stirrups a partial silence, then a mightier roar of anger at once proclaimed and hailed the reappearance of the vidame. Bigoted beyond belief were the mob of Paris of that day, cruel, vengeful, and always athirst for blood; and this man had killed not only their leader but a priest. He had committed sacrilege! What would they do? I could just, by stooping forward, command a side view of the gallery, and the scene passing there was such that I forgot in it our own peril.

For surely in all his reckless life Bezers had never been so emphatically the man for the situa-

tion — had never shown to such advantage as at
this moment when he stood confronting the sea of
faces, the sneer on his lips, a smile in his eyes, and
looked down unblenching, a figure of scorn, on
the men who were literally agape for his life. The
calm defiance of his steadfast look fascinated even
me. Wonder and admiration for the time took
the place of dislike. I could scarcely believe
that there was not some atom of good in this man
so fearless. And no face but one — no face I
think in the world, but one — could have drawn
my eyes from him. But that one face was beside
him. I clutched Marie's arm, and pointed to the
bareheaded figure at Bezers' right hand.

It was Louis himself, our Louis de Pavannes.
But he was changed indeed from the gay cavalier
I remembered, and whom I had last seen riding
down the street at Caylus, smiling back at us, and
waving his adieux to his mistress. Beside the
vidame he had the air of being slight, even short.
The face which I had known so bright and win-
ning, was now white and set. His fair, curling
hair, scarce darker than Croisette's, hung dank,
bedabbled with blood which flowed from a
wound in his head. His sword was gone; his
dress was torn and disordered and covered with
dust. His lips moved. But he held up his head,
he bore himself bravely with it all; so bravely
that I choked, and my heart seemed bursting as I

looked at him standing there forlorn and now unarmed. I knew that Kit seeing him thus would gladly have died with him; and I thanked God she did not see him. Yet there was a quietness in his fortitude which made a great difference between his air and that of Bezers. He lacked, as became one looking unarmed on certain death, the sneer and smile of the giant beside him.

What was the vidame about to do? I shuddered as I asked myself. Not surrender him, not fling him bodily to the people? No, not that. I felt sure he would let no others share his vengeance; that his pride would not suffer that; and even while I wondered the doubt was solved. I saw Bezers raise his hand in a peculiar fashion. Simultaneously a cry rang sharply out above the tumult, and down in headlong charge toward the farther steps came the band of horsemen, who had got clear of the crowd on that side. They were but ten or twelve, but under his eye they charged, as if they had been a thousand. The rabble shrank from the collision, and fled aside. Quick as thought the riders swerved, and, changing their course, galloped through the looser part of the throng, and in a trice drew rein side by side with us, a laugh and a jeer on their reckless lips.

It was neatly done, and while it was being done the vidame and his knot of men, with those who had been searching the building, hurried down the gallery toward us, their rear cleared for the moment by the troopers' feint. The dismounted men came bundling down the steps, their eyes aglow with the war-fire, and got horses as they could. Among them I lost sight of Louis, but perceived him presently, pale and bewildered, mounted behind a trooper. A man sprang up before each of us, too, greeting our appearance merely by a grunt of surprise; for it was no time to ask or answer. The mob was recovering itself, and each moment brought it reinforcements, while its fury was augmented by the trick we had played it, and the prospect of our escape.

We were under forty, all told, and some men were riding double. Bezers' eyes glanced hastily over his array, and lit on us three. He turned and gave some order to his lieutenant. The fellow spurred his horse, a splendid gray, as powerful as his master's, alongside of Croisette, threw his arm around the lad, and dragged him dexterously on to his own crupper. I did not understand the action, but I saw Croisette settle himself behind Blaise Buré, for he it was, and supposed no harm was intended. The next moment we had surged forward, and were swaying to and fro in the midst of the crowd.

What ensued I can not tell. The outlook, so far as I was concerned, was limited to wildly plunging horses—we were in the center of the band—and riders swaying in the saddle, with a glimpse here and there of a fringe of white scowling faces and tossing arms. Once, a lane opening, I saw the vidame's charger—he was in the van—stumble and fall among the crowd, and heard a great shout go up. But Bezers by a mighty effort lifted it to its legs again. And once too, a minute later, those riding on my right swerved outward, and I saw something I never afterward forgot.

It was the body of the coadjutor, lying face upward, the eyes open and the teeth bared in a last spasm. Prostrate on it lay a woman, a young woman, with hair like red gold falling about her neck, and skin like milk. I did not know whether she was alive or dead, but I noticed that one arm stuck out stiffly and the crowd flying before the sudden impact of the horses must have passed over her, even if she had escaped the iron hoofs which followed. Still in the fleeting glance I had of her as my horse bounded aside, I saw no wound or disfigurement. Her one arm was cast about the priest's breast, her face was hidden on it. But for all that, I knew her—knew her, shuddering for the woman whose badges I was even now wearing, whose gift I bore at my side, and I remembered the priest's vaunt of a few hours before, made in her presence, "There is no man in Paris shall thwart me to-night."

It had been a vain boast, indeed! No hand in all that host of thousands was more feeble than his now, for good or ill. No brain more dull, no voice less heeded. A righteous retribution, indeed, had overtaken him. He had died by the sword he had drawn — died, a priest, by violence! The cross he had renounced had crushed him. And all his schemes and thoughts, and no doubt they had been many, had perished with him. It had come to this, only this, the sum of the whole matter, that there was one wicked man the less in Paris — one lump of breathless clay the more.

For her — the woman on his breast — what man can judge a woman, knowing her? And not knowing her, how much less? For the present I put her out of my mind, feeling for the moment faint and cold.

We were clear of the crowd and clattering unmolested down a paved street before I fully recovered from the shock which this sight had caused me. Wonder whither we were going took its place. To Bezers' house? My heart sank at the prospect if that were so. Before I thought of an alternative a gateway, flanked by huge, round towers appeared before us, and we pulled up suddenly, a confused jostling mass in the narrow way; while some words passed between the vidame and the captain of the guard. A pause of several minutes followed; and then the gates rolled slowly

14

open, and two by two we passed under the arch. Those gates might have belonged to a fortress or a prison, a dungeon or a palace, for all I knew.

They led, however, to none of these, but to an open space, dirty and littered with rubbish, marked by a hundred ruts and tracks, and fringed with disorderly cabins and makeshift booths. And beyond this — oh, ye gods! the joy of it — beyond this, which we crossed at a rapid trot, lay the open country!

The transition and relief were so wonderful that I shall never forget them. I gazed on the wide landscape before me, lying quiet and peaceful in the sunlight, and could scarely believe in my happiness. I drew the fresh air into my lungs. I threw up my sheathed sword and caught it again in a frenzy of delight, while the gloomy men about me smiled at my enthusiasm. I felt the horse beneath me move once more like a thing of life. No enchanter with his wand, not Merlin nor Virgil, could have made a greater change in my world than had the captain of the gate with his simple key! Or so it seemed to me in the first moments of freedom and escape — of removal from those loathsome streets.

I looked back at Paris, at the cloud of smoke which hung over the towers and roofs, and it seemed to me the canopy of hell itself. I fancied that my head still rang with the cries and screams and curses, the sounds of death. In very fact I could hear the dull reports of firearms near the Louvre, and the jangle of the bells. Country-folk were congregated at the cross-roads and in the villages, listening and gazing; asking timid questions of the more good-natured among us, and showing that the rumor of the dreadful work doing in the town had somehow spread abroad. And this though I learned afterward that the keys of the city had been taken the night before to the king, and that, except a party with the Duke of Guise, who had left at eight in pursuit of Montgomery and some of the Protestants — lodgers, happily for themselves, in the Faubourg St. Germain — no one had left the town before ourselves.

While I am speaking of our departure from Paris, I may say what I have to say of the dreadful excesses of those days, ay, and of the following days; excesses of which France is now ashamed, and for which she blushed even before the accession of his late majesty. I am sometimes asked, as one who witnessed them, what I think, and I answer that it was not our country which was to blame. A something besides Queen Catherine de' Medici had been brought from Italy forty years before, a something invisible but very powerful; a spirit of cruelty and treachery. In Italy it had done small harm. But grafted on

French daring and recklessness, and the rougher and more soldierly manners of the north, this spirit of intrigue proved capable of very dreadful things. For a time, until it wore itself out, it was the curse of France. Two Dukes of Guise, Francis and Henry, a cardinal of Guise, the Prince of Condé, Admiral Coligny, King Henry III. —all these the foremost men of their day—died by assassination within little more than a quarter of a century, to say nothing of the Prince of Orange and King Henry the Great.

Then mark—a most curious thing—the extreme youth of those who were in this business. France, subject to the queen-mother, of course, was ruled at the time by boys scarce out of their tutors' hands. They were mere lads, hot-blooded, reckless nobles, ready for any wild brawl, without forethought or prudence. Of the four Frenchmen who it is thought took the leading parts, one, the king, was twenty-two; monsieur, his brother, was only twenty; the Duke of Guise was twenty-one! Only the Marshal de Tavannes was of mature age. For the other conspirators, for the queen-mother, for her advisers Retz and Nevers and Birague, they were Italians; and Italy may answer for them if Florence, Mantua, and Milan care to raise the glove.

To return to our journey. A league from the town we halted at a large inn, and some of us dismounted. Horses were brought out to fill the places of those lost or left behind, and Buré had food served to us. We were famished and exhausted, and ate it ravenously, as if we could never have enough.

The vidame sat his horse apart, served by his page. I stole a glance at him, and it struck me that even on his iron nature the events of the night had made some impression. I read, or thought I read, in his countenance signs of emotions not quite in accordance with what I knew of him — emotions strange and varied. I could almost have sworn that as he looked at us a flicker of kindliness lit up his stern and cruel gloom; I could almost have sworn he smiled with a curious sadness. As for Louis, riding with a squad who stood in a different part of the yard, he did not see us; had not yet seen us at all. His side face, turned toward me, was pale and sad, his manner preoccupied, his mien rather sorrowful than downcast. He was thinking, I judged, as much of the many brave men who had yesterday been his friends — companions at board and play-table — as of his own fate. When we presently, at a signal from Buré, took to the road again, I asked no permission, but thrusting my horse forward, rode to his side as he passed through the gateway.

CHAPTER XI.

A NIGHT OF SORROW.

"Louis! Louis!"

He turned with a start at the sound of my voice, joy and bewilderment — and no wonder — in his countenance. He had not supposed us to be within a hundred leagues of him. And lo! here we were, knee to knee, hand meeting hand in a long grasp, while his eyes, to which tears sprang unbidden, dwelt on my face as though they could read in it the features of his sweetheart. Some one had furnished him with a hat, and enabled him to put his dress in order, and wash his wound, which was very slight, and these changes had improved his appearance; so that the shadow of grief and despondency passing for a moment from him in the joy of seeing me, he looked once more his former self, as he had looked in the old days of Caylus on his return from hawking, or from some boyish escapade among the hills. Only, alas! he wore no sword.

"And now tell me all," he cried, after his first exclamation of wonder had found vent. "How on earth do you come here? Here, of all places, and by my side? Is all well at Caylus? Surely mademoiselle is not —"

"Mademoiselle is well, perfectly well! And thinking of you, I swear!" I answered passionately. "For us," I went on, eager for a moment to escape that subject — how could I talk of it in the daylight and under strange eyes? — "Marie and Croisette are behind. We left Caylus eight days ago. We reached Paris yesterday evening. We have not been to bed. We have passed, Louis, such a night as I never —"

He stopped me with a gesture. "Hush!" he said, raising his hand. "Don't speak of it, Anne!" and I saw that the fate of his friends was still too recent, the horror of his awakening to those dreadful sights and sounds was still too vivid for him to bear reference to them. Yet after riding for a time in silence — though his lips moved — he asked me again what had brought us up.

"We came to warn you — of him," I answered, pointing to the solitary, moody figure of the vidame, who was riding ahead of the party. "He — he said that Kit should never marry you, and boasted of what he would do to you, and frightened her. So, learning he was going to Paris, we followed him — to put you on your guard, you know." And I briefly sketched our adventures, and the strange circumstances and mistakes which had delayed us hour after hour, through all that strange night, until the time had gone by when we could do good.

His eyes glistened and his color rose as I told the story. He wrung my hand warmly, and looked back to smile at Marie and Croisette. "It was like you!" he ejaculated, with emotion. "It was like her cousins! Brave, brave lads! The vicomte will live to be proud of you. Some day you will all do great things. I say it!"

"But, oh, Louis!" I exclaimed, sorrowfully, though my heart was bounding with pride at his words, "if we had only been in time! If we had only come to you two hours earlier!"

"You would have spoken to little purpose, then, I fear," he replied, shaking his head. "We were given over as a prey to the enemy. Warnings? We had warnings in plenty. De Rosny warned us, and we scoffed at him. The king's eye warned us, and we trusted him. But—" and Louis' form dilated and his hand rose as he went on, and I thought of his cousin's prediction—"it will never be so again in France, Anne! Never! No man will after this trust another! There will be no honor, no faith, no quarter, and no peace. And for the Valois who has done this, the sword will never depart from his house. I believe it! I do believe it!"

How truly he spoke we know now. For two-and-twenty years after that 24th of August, 1572, the sword was scarcely laid aside in France for a single month. In the streets of

Paris, at Arques, and Coutras, and Ivry, blood flowed like water, that the blood of the St. Bartholomew might be forgotten — that blood which, by the grace of God, Navarre saw fall from the dice-box on the eve of the massacre. The last of the Valois passed to the vaults of St. Denis, and a greater king, the first of all Frenchmen, alive or dead, the bravest, gayest, wisest of the land, succeeded him; yet even he had to fall by the knive, in a moment most unhappy for his country, before France, horror-stricken, put away the treachery and evil from her.

Talking with Louis as we rode, it was not unnatural — nay, it was the natural result of the situation — that I should avoid one subject. Yet that subject was the uppermost in my thoughts. What were the vidame's intentions? What was the meaning of this strange journey? What was to be Louis' fate? I shrank with good reason from asking him these questions. There could be so little room for hope, even after that smile which I had seen Bezers smile, that I dared not dwell upon them. I should but torture him and myself.

So it was he who first spoke about it. Not at that time, but after sunset, when the dusk had fallen upon us, and found us still plodding southward with tired horses; a link outwardly like other links in the long chain of riders, toiling onward. Then he said, suddenly, "Do you know whither we are going, Anne?"

I started, and found myself struggling with a strange confusion before I could reply. "Home," I suggested at random.

"Home? No. And yet nearly home. To Cahors," he answered with an odd quietude. "Your home, my boy, I shall never see again. Nor Kit! Nor my own Kit! It was the first time I had heard him call her by the fond name we used ourselves. And the pathos in his tone as of the past, not the present, as of pure memory —I was very thankful that I could not in the dusk see his face—shook my self-control. I wept. "Nay, my lad," he went on, speaking softly and leaning from his saddle so that he could lay his hand on my shoulder, "we are all men together. We must be brave. Tears can not help us, so we should leave them to the — women."

I cried more passionately at that. Indeed his own voice quavered over the last word. But in a moment he was talking to me coolly and quietly. I had muttered something to the effect that the vidame would not dare—it would be too public.

"There is no question of daring in it," he replied. "And the more public it is, the better he will like it. They have dared to take thousands of lives since yesterday. There is no one to call

him to account since the king—our king forsooth!
—has declared every Huguenot an outlaw, to be
killed wherever he be met with. No, when Bezers
disarmed me yonder," he pointed as he spoke to
his wound, "I looked of course for instant death,
Anne. I saw blood in his eyes! But he did not
strike."

"Why not?" I asked in suspense.

"I can only guess," Louis answered with a
sigh. "He told me that my life was in his hands,
but that he should take it at his own time.
Further, that if I would not give my word to go
with him without trying to escape, he would
throw me to those howling dogs outside. I gave
my word. We are on the road together. And
oh, Anne! yesterday, only yesterday, at this time
I was riding home with Teligny from the Louvre,
where we had been playing at paume with the
king! And the world—the world was very fair."

"I saw you, or rather Croisette did," I muttered, as his sorrow, not for himself but his
friends, forced him to stop. "Yet how, Louis,
do you know that we are going to Cahors?"

"He told me, as we passed through the gates,
that he was appointed Lieutenant-Governor of
Quercy to carry out the edict against the religion.
Do you not see, Anne?" my companion added
bitterly. "To kill me at once was too small a
revenge for him! He must torture me—or rather

he would if he could — by the pains of anticipation. Besides, my execution will so finely open
his bed of justice. Bah!" and Pavannes raised
his head proudly, "I fear him not! I fear him
not a jot!"

For a moment he forgot Kit, the loss of his
friends, his own doom. He snapped his fingers in
derision of his foe.

But my heart sank miserably. The vidame's
rage, I remembered, had been directed rather
against my cousin than her lover, and now by the
light of his threats I read Bezers' purpose more
clearly than Louis could. His aim was to punish
the woman who had played with him. To do so
he was bringing her lover from Paris that he might
execute him, *after giving her notice!* That
was it; after giving her notice, it might be in
her very presence! He would lure her to Cahors,
and then —

I shuddered. I well might feel that a precipice
was opening at my feet. There was something in
the plan so devilish, yet so accordant with those
stories I had heard of the Wolf, that I felt no
doubt of my insight. I read his evil mind, and
saw in a moment why he had troubled himself
with us. He hoped to draw mademoiselle to
Cahors by our means.

Of course I said nothing of this to Louis. I hid
my feelings as well as I could. But I vowed a

great vow that at the eleventh hour we would
balk the vidame. Surely if all else failed we
could kill him, and, though we died ourselves,
spare Kit this ordeal. My tears were dried up as
by a fire. My heart burned with a great and noble
rage; or so it seemed to me.

I do not think that there was ever any journey
so strange as this one of ours. We met with the
same incidents which had pleased us on the road
to Paris. But their novelty was gone. Gone, too,
were the cosy chats with old rogues of landlords
and good-natured dames. We were traveling
now in such force that our coming was rather a
terror to the innkeeper than a boon. How much
the Lieutenant-Governor of Quercy, going down
to his province, requisitioned in the king's name,
and for how much he paid, we could only judge
from the gloomy looks which followed us as we
rode away each morning. Such looks were not
solely due, I fear, to the news from Paris, although
for some time we were the first bearers of the
tidings.

Presently, on the third day of our journey I
think, couriers from the court passed us, and
henceforth forestalled us. One of these messen-
gers — who I learned from the talk about me was
bound for Cahors with letters for the lieutenant-
governor and the count-bishop — the vidame inter-
viewed and stopped. How it was managed I do

not know, but I fear the count-bishop never got his letters, which I fancy would have given him some joint authority. Certainly we left the messenger—a prudent fellow with a care for his skin —in comfortable quarters at Limoges, whence I do not doubt he presently returned to Paris at his leisure.

The strangeness of the journey, however, arose from none of these things, but from the relations of our party to one another. After the first day we four rode together, unmolested, so long as we kept near the center of the straggling cavalcade. The vidame always rode alone, and in front, brooding with bent head and somber face over his revenge, as I supposed. He would ride in this fashion, speaking to no one and giving no orders, for a day together. At times I came near to pitying him. He had loved Kit in his masterful way, the way of one not wont to be thwarted, and he had lost her—lost her, whatever might happen. He would get nothing after all by his revenge; nothing but ashes in the mouth. And so I saw in softer moments something inexpressibly melancholy in that solitary giant-figure pacing always alone.

He seldom spoke to us. More rarely to Louis. When he did, the harshness of his voice and his cruel eyes betrayed the gloomy hatred in which he held him. At meals he ate at one end of the table; we four at the other, as three of us had done on that first evening in Paris. And sometimes the covert looks, the grim sneer he shot at his rival — his prisoner — made me shiver even in the sunshine. Sometimes, on the other hand, when I took him unawares, I found an expression on his face I could not read.

I told Croisette, but warily, my suspicions of his purpose. He heard me, less astounded to all appearance than I had expected. Presently I learned the reason. He had his own view. "Do you not think it possible, Anne," he suggested timidly — we were of course alone at the time — "that he thinks to make Louis resign mademoiselle?"

"Resign her!" I exclaimed, obtusely. "How?"

"By giving him a choice — you understand?"

I did understand — I saw it in a moment. I had been dull not to see it before. Bezers might put it in this way: Let M. de Pavannes resign his mistress and live, or die and lose her.

"I see," I answered. "But Louis would not give her up. Not to him!"

"He would lose her either way," Croisette answered in a low tone. "That is not, however, the worst of it. Louis is in his power. Suppose he thinks to make Kit the arbiter, Anne, and puts Louis up to ransom, setting Kit for the price? And gives her the option of accepting himself, and saving Louis' life; or refusing, and leaving Louis to die?"

"St. Croix!" I exclaimed, fiercely, "he would not be so base!" And yet was not even this better than the blind vengeance I had myself attributed to him?

"Perhaps not," Croisette answered, while he gazed onward through the twilight. We were at the time the foremost of the party save the vidame; and there was nothing to interrupt our view of his gigantic figure, as he moved on alone before us with bowed shoulders. "Perhaps not," Croisette repeated, thoughtfully. "Sometimes I think we do not understand him; and that after all there may be worse people in the world than Bezers."

I looked hard at the lad, for that was not what I had meant. "Worse?" I said. "I do not think so. Hardly!"

"Yes, worse," he replied, shaking his head. "Do you remember lying under the curtain in the box-bed at Mirepoix's?"

"Of course I do! Do you think I shall ever forget it?"

"And Madame d'O coming in?"

"With the coadjutor?" I said with a shudder. "Yes."

"No, the second time," he answered, "when she came back alone. It was pretty dark, you remember, and Madame de Pavannes was at the window, and her sister did not see her?"

"Well, well, I remember," I said, impatiently. I knew from the tone of his voice that he had something to tell me about Madame d'O, and I was not anxious to hear it. I shrank, as a wounded man shrinks from the cautery, from hearing anything about that woman; herself so beautiful, yet moving in an atmosphere of suspicion and horror. Was it shame or fear, or some chivalrous feeling having its origin in that moment when I had fancied myself her knight? I am not sure, for I had not made up my mind, even now, whether I ought to pity or detest her; whether she had made a tool of me, or I had been false to her.

"She came up to the bed, you remember, Anne?" Croisette went on. "You were next to her. She saw you indistinctly, and took you for her sister. And then I sprang from the bed."

"I know you did!" I exclaimed, sharply. All this time I had forgotten that grievance. "You nearly frightened her out of her wits, St. Croix. I can not think what possessed you — why you did it!"

"To save your life, Anne," he answered, solemnly, "and her from a crime; an unutterable, an unnatural crime. She had come back to — I can hardly tell it to you — to murder her

15

sister. You start. You do not believe me. It sounds too horrible. But I could see better than you could. She was exactly between you and the light. I saw the knife raised. I saw her wicked face. If I had not startled her as I did, she would have stabbed you. She dropped the knife on the floor, and I picked it up and have it. See!"

I looked furtively and turned away again, shivering. "Why," I muttered, "why did she do it?"

"She had failed, you know, to get her sister back to Pavannes' house, where she would have fallen an easy victim. Bezers, who knew Madame d'O, prevented that. Then that fiend slipped back with her knife, thinking that in the common butchery the crime would be overlooked and never investigated, and that Mirepoix would be silent."

I said nothing. I was stunned. Yet I believed the story. When I went over the facts in my mind I found that a dozen things, overlooked at the time and almost forgotten in the hurry of events, sprang up to confirm it. M. de Pavannes'—the other M. de Pavannes'—suspicions had been well founded. Worse than Bezers was she? Ay! worse a hundred times. As much worse as treachery ever is than violence, as the pitiless fraud of the serpent is baser than the rage of the wolf.

"I thought," Croisette added, softly, not looking at me, "when I discovered that you had gone
off with her, that I should never see you again,
Anne. I gave you up for lost. The happiest
moment of my life, I think, was when I saw you
come back."

"Croisette," I whispered, piteously, my cheeks
burning, "let us never speak of her again."

And we never did — for years. But how strange
is life! She and the wicked man with whom her
fate seemed bound up had just crossed our lives
when their own were at the darkest. They clashed
with us, and, strangers and boys as we were, we
ruined them. I have often asked myself what
would have happened to me had I met her at some
earlier and less stormy period — in the brilliance
of her beauty? And I find but one answer. I
should bitterly have rued the day. Providence
was good to me. Such men and such women, we
may believe, have ceased to exist now. They
flourished in those miserable days of war and
divisions, and passed away with them like the
foul night-birds of the battle-field.

To return to our journey. In the morning
sunshine one could not but be cheerful, and think
good things possible. The worst trial I had came
with each sunset. For then — we generally rode
late into the evening — Louis sought my side to
talk to me of his sweetheart. And how he would

talk of her! How many thousand messages he
gave me for her! How often he recalled old days
among the hills, with each laugh, and jest, and
incident, when we five had been as children!
until I would wonder passionately, the tears running down my face in the darkness, how he could
—how he could talk of her in that quiet voice
which betrayed no rebellion ag inst fate, no cursing of Providence! How he could plan for her
and think of her when she should be alone!

Now I understand it. He was still laboring
under the shock of his friends' murder. He was
still partially stunned. Death seemed natural
and familiar to him, as to one who had seen his
allies and companions perish without warning or
preparation. Death had come to be normal to
him, life the exception; as I have known it seem
to a child brought face to face with a corpse for
the first time.

One afternoon a strange thing happened. We
could see the Auvergne hills at no great distance
on our left — the Puy de Dôme above them — and
we four were riding together. We had fallen —
an unusual thing — to the rear of the party. Our
road at the moment was a mere track running
across moorland, sprinkled here and there with
gorse and brushwood. The main company had
straggled on out of sight. There were but half a
dozen riders to be seen an eighth of a league

before us, a couple almost as far behind. I looked every way with a sudden surging of the heart. For the first time the possibility of flight occurred to me. The rough Auvergne hills were within reach. Supposing we could get a lead of a quarter of a league; we could hardly be caught before darkness came and covered us. Why should we not put spurs to our horses and ride off?

"Impossible!" said Pavannes quietly, when I spoke.

"Why?" I asked with warmth.

"Firstly," he replied, "because I have given my word to go with the vidame to Cahors."

My face flushed hotly. But I cried, "What of that? You were taken by treachery. Your safe conduct was disregarded. Why should you be scrupulous? Your enemies are not. This is folly."

"I think not. Nay," Louis answered, shaking his head, "you would not do it yourself in my place."

"I think I should," I stammered awkwardly.

"No, you would not, lad," he said, smiling. "I know you too well. But if I would do it, it is impossible." He turned in the saddle, and shading his eyes with his hand from the level rays of the sun, looked back intently. "It is as I thought," he continued. "One of those men is riding grey Margot, which Buré said yesterday was the fastest mare in the troop. And the man on her is a light weight. The other fellow has that Norman bay horse we were looking at this morning. It is a trap laid by Bezers, Anne. If we turned aside a dozen yards, those two would be after us like the wind.''

"Do you mean," I cried, "that Bezers has drawn his men forward on purpose?''

"Precisely," was Louis' answer. "That is the fact. Nothing would please him better than to take my honor first and my life afterward. But, thank God, only the one is in his power.''

And when I came to look at the horsemen, immediately before us, they confirmed Louis' view. They were the best mounted of the party —all men of light weight, too. One or other of them was constantly looking back. As night fell they closed in upon us with their usual care. When Buré joined us there was a gleam of intelligence in his bold eyes, a flash of conscious trickery. He knew that we had found him out, and cared nothing for it.

And the others cared nothing. But the thought that if left to myself I should have fallen into the vidame's cunning trap filled me with new hatred toward him; such hatred and such fear, for there was humiliation mingled with them, as I had scarcely felt before. I brooded over this, barely noticing what passed in our company for hours — nay, not until the next day when, toward evening, the cry arose around me that we were in sight of Cahors. Yes, there it lay below us, in its shallow basin, surrounded by gentle hills. The domes of the cathedral, the towers of the Vallandré Bridge, the bend of the Lot, where its stream embraces the town — I knew them all. Our long journey was over.

And I had but one idea. I had some time before communicated to Croisette the desperate design I had formed — to fall upon Bezers and kill him in the midst of his men — in the last resort. Now the time had come if the thing was ever to be done, if we had not left it too long already. And I looked about me. There was some confusion and jostling as we halted on the brow of the hill, while two men were dispatched ahead to announce the governor's arrival, and Buré, with half a dozen spears, rode out as an advance guard.

The road where we stood was narrow, a shallow cutting winding down the declivity of the hills. The horses were tired. It was a bad time and place for my design, and only the coming night was in my favor. But I was desperate.

Yet before I moved or gave a signal which nothing could recall, I scanned the landscape eagerly, scrutinizing in turn the small, rich plain below us, warmed by the last rays of the sun, the bare hills here glowing, there dark, the scattered wood-clumps and spinneys that filled the angles of the river, even the dusky line of holm-oaks that crowned the ridge beyond, Caylus-way. So near our own country there might be help! If the messenger whom we had dispatched to the vicomte before leaving home had reached him, our uncle might have returned, and even be in Cahors to meet us.

But no party appeared in sight, and I saw no place where an ambush could be lying. I remembered that no tidings of our present plight or of what had happened could have reached the vicomte. The hope faded out of life as soon as despair had given it birth. We must fend for ourselves and for Kit.

That was my justification. I leaned from my saddle toward Croisette — I was riding by his side — and muttered, as I felt my horses head and settled myself firmly in the stirrups. "You remember what I said? Are you ready?"

He looked at me in a startled way, with a face showing white in the shadow, and from me to the one solitary figure seated like a pillar a score of paces in front, with no one between us and it. "There need be but two of us," I muttered, loosening my sword. "Shall it be you or Marie? The others must leap their horses out of the road in the confusion, cross the river at the Arembal

Ford if they are not overtaken, and make for Caylus."

He hesitated. I do not know whether it had anything to do with his hesitation that at that moment the cathedral bell in the town below us began to ring slowly for vespers. Yes, he hesitated. He—a Caylus. Turning to him again, I repeated my question impatiently. "Which shall it be? A moment, and we shall be moving on, and it will be too late."

He laid his hand hurriedly on my bridle, and began a rambling answer. Rambling as it was I gathered his meaning. It was enough for me. I cut him short with one word of fiery indignation, and turned to Marie and spoke quickly.

"Will you, then?" I said.

But Marie shook his head in perplexity, and answering little, said the same.

So it happened a second time.

Strange! Yet strange as it seemed, I was not greatly surprised. Under other circumstances I should have been beside myself with anger at the defection. Now I felt as if I had half expected it, and without further words of reproach I dropped my head and gave it up. I passed again into the stupor of endurance. The vidame was too strong for me. It was useless to fight against him. We were under the spell. When the troop moved forward, I went with them, silent and apathetic.

We passed through the gate of Cahors, and no doubt the scene was worthy of note, but I had only a listless eye for it — much such an eye as a man about to be broken on the wheel must have for that curious instrument, supposing him never to have seen it before. The whole population had come out to line the streets through which we rode, and stood gazing, with scarcely veiled looks of apprehension, at the procession of troopers and the stern face of the new governor.

We dismounted passively in the courtyard of the castle, and were for going in together, when Buré intervened. "M. de Pavannes," he said, pushing rather rudely between us, "will sup alone to-night. For you, gentlemen, this way, if you please."

I went without remonstrance. What was the use? I was conscious that the vidame from the top of the stairs leading to the grand entrance was watching us with a wolfish glare in his eyes. I went quietly. But I heard Croisette urging something with passionate energy.

We were led through a low doorway to a room on the ground floor, a place very like a cell. Here we took our meal in silence. When it was over I flung myself on one of the beds prepared for us, shrinking from my companions rather in misery than in resentment.

No explanation had passed between us. Still

I knew that the other two from time to time eyed me doubtfully. I feigned therefore to be asleep, but I heard Buré enter to bid us good-night, and see that we had not escaped. And I was conscious, too, of the question Croisette put to him, "Does M. de Pavannes lie alone to-night, Buré?"

"Not entirely," the captain answered, with gloomy meaning. Indeed he seemed in bad spirits himself, or tired. "The vidame is anxious for his soul's welfare, and sends a priest to him."

They sprang to their feet at that. But the light and its bearer, who so far recovered himself as to chuckle at his master's pious thought, had disappeared. They were left to pace the room, and reproach themselves and curse the vidame in an agony of late repentance. Not even Marie could find a loop-hole of escape from here. The door was double-locked; the windows so barred that a cat could scarcely pass through them; the walls were of solid masonry.

Meanwhile I lay and feigned sleep, and lay feigning through long, long hours, though my heart like theirs throbbed in response to the dull hammering that presently began without, and not far from us, and lasted until daybreak. From our windows, set low and facing a wall, we could see nothing. But we could guess what the noise meant, the dull, earthy thuds when posts were set in the ground; the brisk, wooden clattering when one plank was laid to another. We could not see the progress of the work, or hear the voices of the workmen, or catch the glare of their lights, but we knew what they were doing. They were raising the scaffold.

CHAPTER XII.

1 WAS too weary with riding to go entirely
without sleep. And, moreover, it is anxiety and
the tremor of excitement which make the pillow
sleepless, not, heaven be thanked, sorrow. God
made man to lie awake and hope, but never to
lie awake and grieve. An hour or two before
daybreak I fell asleep, utterly worn out. When
I awoke the sun was high and shining slantwise
on our window. The room was gay with the
morning rays, and soft with the morning freshness, and I lay awhile, my cheek on my hand,
drinking in the cheerful influence as I had done
many and many a day in our room at Caylus. It
was the touch of Marie's hand, laid timidly on
my arm, which roused me with a shock to con-
sciousness. The truth broke upon me. I remembered where we were, and what was before us.
"Will you get up Anne?" Croisette said. "The
vidame has sent for us."

I got to my feet and buckled on my sword.
Croisette was leaning against the wall, pale and
downcast. Buré filled the open doorway, his
feathered cap in his hand, a queer smile on his
face. "You are a good sleeper, young gentle-

man," he said. "You should have a good con-
science."

"Better than yours, no doubt!" I retorted,
"or your master's."

He shrugged his shoulders, and, bidding us by
a sign to follow him, led the way through several
gloomy passages. At the end of these a flight of
stone steps, leading upward, seemed to promise
something better; and true enough, the door at the
top being opened, the murmur of a crowd reached
our ears, with a burst of sunlight and warmth.
We were in a lofty room, with walls in some places
painted and elsewhere hung with tapestry; well
lighted by three old pointed windows reaching to
the rush-covered floor. The room was large, set
here and there with stands of arms, and had a dais
with a raised carved chair at one end. The ceiling was of blue, with gold stars set about it.
Seeing this, I remembered the place. I had been
in it once, years ago, when I had attended the
vicomte on a state visit to the governor. Ah!
that the vicomte were here now!

I advanced to the middle window, which was
open. Then I started back, for outside was the
scaffold built level with the floor, and rush-covered like it! Two or three people were lounging
on it. My eyes sought Louis among the group,
but in vain. He was not there; and while I
looked for him, I heard a noise behind me,

and he came in, guarded by four soldiers with pikes.

His face was pale and grave, but perfectly composed. There was a wistful look in his eyes indeed, as if he were thinking of something or some one far away — Kit's face on the sunny hills of Quercy where he had ridden with her, perhaps; a look which seemed to say that the doings here were nothing to him, and the parting was yonder where she was. But his bearing was calm and collected, his step firm and fearless. When he saw us, indeed his face lightened a moment and he greeted us cheerfully, even acknowledging Buré's salutation with dignity and good temper. Croisette sprang toward him impulsively, and cried his name — Croisette ever the first to speak. But before Louis could grasp his hand, the door at the bottom of the hall was swung open, and the vidame came hurriedly in.

He was alone. He glanced round, his forbidding face, which was somewhat flushed as if by haste, wearing a scowl. Then he saw us, and, nodding haughtily, strode up the floor, his spurs clanking heavily on the boards. He gave us no greeting, but by a short word dismissed Buré and the soldiers to the lower end of the room. And then he stood and looked at us four, but principally at his rival; and looked — and looked with eyes of smoldering hate. And there was a silence, a long silence, while the murmur of the crowd came almost cheerfully through the window, and the sparrows under the eaves chirped and twittered, and the heart that throbbed least painfully was, I do believe, Louis de Pavannes'!

At last Bezers broke the silence.

"M. de Pavannes," he began, speaking hoarsely, yet concealing all passion under a cynical smile and a mock politeness, "M. de Pavannes, I hold the king's commission to put to death all the Huguenots within my province of Quercy. Have you anything to say, I beg, why I should not begin with you? Or do you wish to return to the church?"

Louis shrugged his shoulders as in contempt, and held his peace. I saw his captor's great hands twitch convulsively at this, but still the vidame mastered himself, and when he spoke again he spoke slowly. "Very well," he continued, taking no heed of us, the silent witnesses of this strange struggle between the two men, but eyeing Louis only. "You have wronged me more than any man alive. Alive or dead! or dead! You have thwarted me, M. de Pavannes, and taken from me the woman I loved. Six days ago I might have killed you. I had it in my power. I had but to leave you to the rabble, remember, and you would have been rotting at Montfaucon to-day, M. de Pavannes."

"That is true," said Louis, quietly. "Why so many words?"

But the vidame went on as if he had not heard. "I did not leave you to them," he resumed, "and yet I hate you — more than I ever hated any man yet, and I am not apt to forgive. But now the time has come, sir, for my revenge! The oath I swore to your mistress a fortnight ago I will keep to the letter. I — silence, babe!" he thundered, turning suddenly, "or I will keep my word with you, too!"

Croisette had muttered something, and this had drawn on him the glare of Bezers' eyes. But the threat was effectual. Croisette was silent. The two were left henceforth to one another.

Yet the vidame seemed to be put out by the interruption. Muttering a string of oaths, he strode from us to the window and back again. The cool cynicism with which he was wont to veil his anger and impose on other men, while it heightened the effect of his ruthless deeds, in part fell from him. He showed himself as he was — masterful and violent, hating with all the strength of a turbulent nature which had never known a check. I quailed before him myself. I confess it.

"Listen!" he continued harshly, coming back and taking his place in front of us at last, his manner more violent than before the interruption. "I might have left you to die in that hell yonder!

16

And I did not leave you. I had but to hold my hand, and you would have been torn to pieces! The wolf, however, does not hunt with the rats, and a Bezers wants no help in his vengeance from king or *canaille!* When I hunt my enemy down I will hunt him alone, do you hear? And as there is a heaven above me" — he paused a moment — "if I ever meet you face to face again, M. de Pavannes, I will kill you where you stand!"

He paused, and the murmur of the crowd without came to my ears, but mingled with and heightened by some confusion in my thoughts. I struggled feebly with this, seeing a rush of color to Croisette's face, a lightening in his eyes as if a veil had been raised from before them. Some confusion, for I thought I grasped the vidame's meaning; yet there he was still glowering on his victim with the same grim visage, still speaking in the same rough tone. "Listen, M. de Pavannes," he continued, rising to his full height and waving his hand with a certain majesty toward the window — no one had spoken. "The doors are open! Your mistress is at Caylus. The road is clear; go to her. Go to her, and tell her that I have saved your life, and that I gave it to you not out of love, but out of hate! If you had flinched I would have killed you, for so you would have suffered most, M. de Pavannes. As it is, take your life — a gift! and suffer as I should if I were saved and spared by my enemy.

Slowly the full sense of his words came home to me. Slowly, not in its full completeness indeed until I heard Louis in broken phrases, phrases half proud and half humble, thanking him for his generosity. Even then I almost lost the true and wondrous meaning of the thing when I heard his answer. For he cut Pavannes short with bitter caustic gibes, spurned his proffered gratitude with insults, and replied to his acknowledgments with threats.

"Go! go!" he continued to cry violently. "Have I brought you so far safely that you will cheat me of my vengeance at the last, and provoke me to kill you? Away, and take these blind puppies with you! Reckon me as much your enemy now as ever! And if I meet you, be sure you will meet a foe! Begone, M. de Pavannes, begone!"

"But, M. de Bezers," Louis persisted, "hear me. It takes two to—"

"Begone! begone! before we do one another a mischief," cried the vidame furiously. "Every word you say in that strain is an injury to me. It robs me of my vengeance. Go! in God's name!"

And we went; for there was no change, no promise of softening in his malignant aspect as he spoke; nor any as he stood and watched us draw

off slowly from him. We went one by one, each
lingering after the other, striving, out of a natural
desire to thank him, to break through that stern
reserve. But grim and unrelenting, a picture of
scorn to the last, he saw us go.

My latest memory of that strange man — still
fresh after a lapse of two and fifty years — is of
a huge form towering in the gloom below the
state canopy, the sunlight which poured in
through the windows and flooded us, falling short
of him; of a pair of fierce, cross eyes, that seemed
to glow as they covered us; of a lip that curled
as in the enjoyment of some cruel jest. And so
I — and I think each of us four — saw the last of
Raoul de Mar, Vidame de Bezers, in this life.

He was a man whom we can not judge by to-
day's standard; for he was such an one in his
vices and his virtues as the present day does not
know; one who in his time did immense evil —
and, if his friends be believed, little good. But
the evil is forgotten, the good lives. And if all
that good save one act were buried with him, this
one act alone, the act of a French gentleman,
would be told of him — ay! and will be told — as
long as the kingdom of France and the gracious
memory of the late king shall endure.

*　　*　　*　　*　　*　　*　　*　　*

I see again by the simple process of shutting
my eyes, the little party of five — for Jean, our

servant, had rejoined us — who on that summer
day rode over the hills to Caylus, threading the
mazes of the holm-oaks, and galloping down the
rides, and hallooing the hare from her form, but
never pursuing her; arousing the nestling farm-
houses from their sleepy stillness by joyous shout
and laugh, and sniffing, as we climbed the hill-
side again, the scent of the ferns that died,
crushed under our horses' hoofs — died only that
they might add one little pleasure more to the
happiness God had given us. Rare and sweet
indeed are those few days in life when it seems
that all creation lives only that we may have
pleasure in it, and thank God for it. It is well
that we should make the most of them, as we
surely did of that day.

It was nightfall when we reached the edge
of the uplands and looked down on Caylus.
The last rays of the sun lingered with us, but
the valley below was dark; so dark that even
the rock about which our homes clustered
would have been invisible save for the half-
dozen lights that were beginning to twinkle into
being on its summit. A silence fell upon us as
we slowly wended our way down the well-known
path.

All day long we had ridden in great joy; if
thoughtless, yet innocent; if selfish, yet thankful;
and always blithely, with a great exultation and

relief at heart, a great rejoicing for our own sakes and for Kit's.

Now with the nightfall and the darkness, now when we were near our home, and on the eve of giving joy to another, we grew silent. There arose other thoughts — thoughts of all that had happened since we had last ascended that track; and so our minds turned naturally back to him to whom we owed our happiness — to the giant left behind in his pride and power and his loneliness. The others could think of him with full hearts, yet without shame. But I reddened, reflecting how it would have been with us if I had had my way; if I had resorted in my short-sightedness to one last violent, cowardly deed, and killed him, as I had twice wished to do.

Pavannes would then have been lost — almost certainly. Only the vidame with his powerful troop — we never knew whether he had gathered them for that purpose or merely with an eye to his government — could have saved him. And few men, however powerful — perhaps Bezers only of all men in Paris — would have dared to snatch him from the mob when once it had sighted him. I dwell on this now that my grandchildren may take warning by it, though never will they see such days as I have seen.

And so we clattered up the steep street of Caylus with a pleasant melancholy upon us, and passed, not without a more serious thought, the gloomy, frowning portals, all barred and shuttered, of the House of the Wolf, and under the very window, somber and vacant, from which Bezers had incited the rabble in their attack on Pavannes' courier. We had gone by day, and we came back by night. But we had gone trembling, and we came back in joy.

We did not need to ring the great bell. Jean's cry, "Ho! Gate there! Open for my lords!" had scarcely passed his lips before we were admitted. And ere we could mount the ramp, one person outran those who came forth to see what the matter was; one outran Madame Claude, outran old Gil, outran the hurrying servants, and the welcome of the house. I saw a slender figure all in white break away from the little crowd and dart toward us, disclosing as it reached me a face that seemed still whiter than its robes, and yet a face that seemed all eyes — eyes that asked the question the lips could not frame.

I stood aside with a low bow, my hat in my hand; and said, simply — it was the great effect of my life —"*Voilà*, monsieur!"

And then I saw the sun rise in a woman's face.

* * * * * *

The Vidame de Bezers died as he had lived. He was still Governor of Cahors when Henry the

Great attacked it on the night of the 17th of June,
1580. Taken by surprise and wounded in the
first confusion of the assault, he still defended
himself and his charge with desperate courage,
fighting from street to street and house to house
for five nights and as many days. While he lived
Henry's destiny and the fate of France trembled
in the balance. But he fell at length, his brain
pierced by the ball of an arquebuse, and died an
hour before sunset on the 22d of June. The gar-
rison immediately surrendered.

Marie and I were present in this action, on the
side of the King of Navarre, and at the request of
that prince hastened to pay such honors to the
vidame as were due to his renown and might serve
to evince our gratitude. A year later his remains
were removed from Cahors, and laid where they
now rest in his own Abbey Church of Bezers,
under a monument which very briefly tells of his
stormy life and his valor. No matter. He has
small need of a monument whose name lives in
the history of his country, and whose epitaph is
written in the lives of men.

NOTE.— The character and conduct of the Vidame de
Bezers, as they appear in the above memoir, find a par-
allel in an account given by De Thou of one of the most
remarkable incidents in the Massacre of St. Bartholomew: "Amid such examples," he writes, "of the

ferocity of the city, a thing happened worthy to be
related, and which may perhaps in some degree weigh
against these atrocities. There was a deadly hatred,
which up to this time the intervention of their friends
and neighbors had failed to appease, between two men
—Vezins, the lieutenant of Honoratus of Savoy, Mar-
shall Villars, a man notable among the nobility of the
province for his valor, but obnoxious to many owing to
his brutal disposition (ferinâ naturâ), and Regnier, a
young man of like rank and vigor, but of milder character.   When Regnier then, in the middle of that great
uproar, death meeting his eye everywhere, was making
up his mind to the worst, his door was suddenly burst
open, and Vezins, with two other men, stood before him
sword in hand.   Upon this Regnier, assured of death,
knelt down and asked mercy of heaven; but Vezins in a
harsh voice bid him rise from his prayers and mount a
palfrey already standing ready in the street for him.   So
he led Regnier — uncertain for the time whither he was
being taken — out of the city, and put him on his honor
to go with him without trying to escape.   And together,
without pausing on their journey, the two traveled all
the way to Guienne.   During this time Vezins honored
Regnier with very little conversation; but so far cared
for him that food was prepared for him at the inns by
his servants, and so they came to Quercy and the castle
of Regnier.   There Vezins turned to him, and said,
"You know how I have for a long time back sought to
avenge myself on you, and how easily I might now have
done it to the full, had I been willing to use this opportunity. But shame would not suffer it; and besides,

your courage seemed worthy to be set against mine on even terms. Take therefore the life which you owe to my kindness." With much more which the curious will find in the second (folio) volume of De Thou.

THE END.

www.ingramcontent.com/pod-product-compliance
Lightning Source LLC
Chambersburg PA
CBHW032035240626
47154CB00003B/929